W9-ABC-002

The Hills of Homicide

THE HILLS
OF HOMICIDE

Louis L'Amour

CARROLL & GRAF PUBLISHERS, INC.

New York

Contents

The Hills of Homicide

FOREWORD

The stories included in this volume originally appeared a number of years ago. This edition is the first to present these vintage Louis L'Amour works in one collection.

Near the end of the age of the pulp magazine, in 1949, Louis L'Amour, who was then mastering the saga of the American West, tried his hand at another truly American creation—the "hard-boiled" detective story.

The hard-boiled tradition was started in the early twenties in the pages of *Black Mask*, the foremost pulp magazine featuring detective fiction. Carroll John Daly is credited with having written the very first hard-boiled detective story with "The False Burton Combs" which appeared in *Black Mask* in 1922. The mythos of the detective story began to develop and become clearly defined when *Black Mask* published the first of the Race Williams stories by Daly in 1923. The detective story was then instilled with realism and sharp, sustained characterization when Dashiell Hammett became a regular contributor to *Black Mask* with his stories of The Continental Op.

Louis L'Amour, too, wrote for the pages of *Black Mask* and the stories in this collection represent the hard-boiled movement as reflected in the detective fiction of the late forties.

THE PUBLISHERS

THE HILLS
OF HOMICIDE

CHAPTER ONE

The Impossible Murder

The station wagon jolted over a rough place in the black top and I opened my eyes and sat up. Nothing had changed. When you are in the desert you are in the desert and it looks it. We had been driving through the same sort of country when I fell asleep, the big mesa that shouldered against the skyline ahead being the only change.

"Ranagat's right up ahead, about three, four miles." Shanks, who was driving me, was a thin-faced little man who sat sideways in the seat and steered with his left hand on the wheel. "You won't see the town until we get close."

"Near that mesa?"

"Right up against it. Small town, about four hundred people when they're all home. Being off the state highway no tourists ever go there. Nothin' to see, anyway."

"No boothill?" Nearly all of the little mining towns in this section have a boothill, and from the look of them, shooting up your neighbors must have been the outstanding recreation in the old days.

"Oh, sure. Not many in this one, though. About fifteen or twenty with markers, but they buried most of them without any kind of a slab. This boothill couldn't hold a candle to Pioche. Over there they buried seventy-five before the first one died of natural causes."

"Rough place."

"You said it. Speakin' of guys gettin' killed, they had a murder in Ranagat the other night. Old fellow, got more money than you could shake a stick at."

"Murder, you say?"

"Uh-huh. They don't know who done it, yet, but you needn't worry. Old Jerry will catch him. That's Jerry Loftus, the sheriff. He's a smart old coot, rustled a few cows himself in the old days.

13

He can sling a gun, too. Don't think he can't. Not that he looks like much, but he could fool you.''

Shanks put a cigarette between his lips and lit it with a match cupped in his right hand. "Bitner, his name was. That's the dead man, I mean." He jerked his cigarette toward the mesa. "Lived up there.''

"On top?'' From where I sat, the wall of sheer, burnt-red sandstone looked impossible to climb. "How'd he get up there?''

"From Ranagat. That's the joker in this case, mister. Only one way up there, an' that way is in plain sight of most of Ranagat, an' goes right by old Johnny Holben's door. Nobody could ever get up that trail without being seen by Johnny.

"The trail goes up through a cut in the rock, and believe me, it's the only way to get on top. At a wide place in the cut, Johnny Holben has a cabin, an' he's a suspicious old coot. He built there to annoy Bitner because they had it in for each other. Used to be partners, one time. Prospected all this country together an' then set up a company to work their mines. Bitner and Holben, they called it. Things went fine for a while, an' they made a mint of money. Then they had trouble an' split up.''

"Holben kill him?''

"Some folks think so, but others say no. Bitner's got him a niece, a right pretty girl named Karen. She came up here to see him, and two days after she gets here he gets murdered. A lot of folks figure that was a mighty funny thing, her being heiress to all that money, an' everything.''

So there were two other suspects, anyway. That made three. Johnny Holben, Karen Bitner, and my client. "Know a guy named Caronna?''

"Blacky Caronna? Sure.'' Shanks slanted a look at me out of those watchful, curious eyes. I knew he was trying to place me, but so far hadn't an inkling. "You know him?''

"Heard of him.'' It was no use telling Shanks what I had come for. I was here to get information, not give it.

"He's a suspect, too. An' in case you don't know, mister, he's not a nice playmate. I mean, you don't get rough with him. Nobody out here knows much about him, an' he's lived in Ranagat for more than ten years, but he's a bad man to fool with.

If your business is with him, you better forget it unless it's peaceful."

"He's a suspect, you say?"

"Sure. Him an' old Bitner had a fight. An argument, that is. Bitner sure told him off, but nobody knows what it was about but Caronna, an' Blacky just ain't talkin'.

"Caronna is sort of a gambler. Seems to have plenty of money, an' this place he built up here is the finest in town. Rarely has any visitors, an' spends most of his time up there alone except when he's playin' poker.

"The boys found out what he was like when he first came out here. In these Western towns they don't take a man on face value, not even when he's got a face like Blacky Caronna's. Big Sam, a big miner, tangled with him. Sam would weigh about two-fifty, I guess, and all man. That's only a shade more than Caronna.

"They went out behind The Sump, that's a pool hall an' saloon, an' they had it out. Boy, was that a scrap! Prettiest I ever seen. They fit tooth an' toenail for near thirty minutes, but that Caronna is the roughest, dirtiest fighter ever come down the pike. Sam was damn near killed."

"Big guy, you say?"

"Uh-huh. Maybe an inch shorter than you, but wide as a barn door. And I mean a big barn! He's a lot heavier than you, an' never seems to get fat." Shanks glanced at me. "What do you weigh? About one-eighty?"

"Two hundred even."

"You don't say? You must have it packed pretty solid. But don't you have trouble with Caronna. You ain't man enough for it."

That made me remember what the boss said before I left. "His money is as good as anybody's money, but don't you get us into trouble. This Caronna is a tough customer, and plenty smart. He's got a record as long as your arm, but he got out of the rackets with plenty of moola, and that took brains. You go over there and investigate that murder and clear him if you can. But watch him all the time. He's just about as trustworthy as a hungry tiger."

The station wagon rolled down the last incline into the street and rolled to a halt in front of a grey stone building with a weather-beaten sign across the front that said Hotel on one end, and Restaurant on the other.

The one street of the town laid everything out before you for one glance. Two saloons, a garage, a blacksmith shop, three stores, and a café. There were two empty buildings, boarded up now, and beyond them another stone building that was a sheriff's office and jail in one piece.

Shanks dropped my bag into the street and reached out a hand. "That will be three bucks," he said. He was displeased with me. All the way over I had listened, but he had no more idea who I was than the man in the moon.

Two thistle-chinned prospectors who looked as if they had trailed a burro all over the hills were sitting on the porch, chewing. Both of them glanced up and stared at me with idle curiosity.

The lobby was a long, dank room with a soot-blackened fireplace and four or five enormous black leather chairs and a settee, all looking as if they had come across the plains fifty or sixty years ago. On the wall was a mountain lion's head that had been attacked by moths.

A clerk, who was probably no youngster when they opened the hotel in '67, got up from a squeaky chair and shoved the register at me. I signed my name and, taking the key, went up the stairs. Inside the room I waited just long enough to take my .45 Colt out of the bag and shove it behind my belt under my shirt. Then I started for the sheriff's office. By the time I had gone the two blocks that comprised the full length of the street, everyone in town knew me by sight.

Jerry Loftus was seated behind a rolltop desk with both feet on the desk and his thumbs hooked in the armholes of his vest. His white, flat-crowned hat was shoved back on his head, and his hair and mustache were as white as the hat. He wore cowboy boots with spurs, and a six-shooter in an open-top holster.

Flipping open my wallet I laid it in front of him with my badge and credentials showing. He glanced down at them without moving a hand, then looked up at me.

"Private detective? Who sent for you?"

"Caronna."

"He's worried, then. What do you aim to do, son?"

"Look around. My orders are to investigate the crime, find evidence to clear him, and so get you off his back. From the sound of it," I was fishing for information, "he didn't seem to believe anybody around here would mind if he was sentenced or not. Guilty or not."

"He's right. Nothing against him myself. Plays a good hand of poker, pays when he loses, collects when he wins. Maybe he buys a little highgrade once in a while, but while the mine owners wish we would put a stop to it, we don't figure that what gold ore a man can smuggle out of a mine is enough to worry about.

"All these holes around here strike pockets of rich ore from time to time. Most of the mines pay off pretty well, anyway, but when they strike that wire gold, the boys naturally get away with what they can.

"The mines all have a change room where the miners take off their diggin' clothes, walk naked for their shower, then out on the other side for their street clothes, but men bein' what they are, they find ways to get out with some gold.

"Naturally, that means they have to have a buyer. Caronna seems to be the man. I don't know that, but I never asked no questions, either."

"Would you mind giving me the lowdown on this killing?"

"Not at all." Loftus shifted his thumbs to his vest pockets. "Pull up a chair an' set. No, not there. Move left a mite. Ain't exactly safe to get between me an' that spittoon."

He chewed thoughtfully for a few minutes. "Murdered man is Jack Bitner, a cantankerous old cuss, wealthy as all get-out. Mine owner now, used to be a prospector. Hard-headed as a blind mule and rough as a chapped lip. Almost seventy, but fit to live twenty years more, ornery as he was. Lived up yonder on the mesa."

Loftus chewed, spat, and continued. "Found dead Monday morning by his niece. Karen Bitner. Killed sometime Sunday night, seems like. Stabbed three times in the back with a knife while settin' at the table.

"Only had two visitors Sunday night. Karen Bitner an' Blacky

Caronna. She went up to see the old man about five of the evenin', claims she left him feelin' right pert. Caronna headed up that way about eight, still light at that hour, an' then says he changed his mind about seein' the old man without a witness, an' came back without ever gettin' to the cabin.

"Only other possible suspect is Johnny Holben. Those two old roosters been spittin' an' snarlin' for the last four years, an' both of them made threats.

"Johnny lives on the trail to the mesa, an' he's got ears like a skittish rabbit an' eyes like a cat. Johnny saw those two go up an' he seen 'em come back, an' he'll take oath nobody else went up that trail. Any jury of folks from around Ranagat would take his word for it that a gopher couldn't go up that trail without Johnny knowin' it. As for himself, Johnny swears he ain't been on the mesa in six years.

"All three had motives, all three had opportunity. Any one of the three could have done it if they got behind Bitner, an' that's what makes me suspicion the girl. I don't believe that suspicious old devil would let any man get behind him."

"Caronna can't clear the girl, then? If he had gone up to the house and found the old man alive, she'd be in the clear."

"That's right. But he says he didn't go to the house, an' we can't prove it one way or another. The way it is, we're stuck. If you can figure some way to catch the guilty man, you'd be a help." Jerry Loftus rolled his quid in his jaws and glanced at me sharply. "You come up here to find evidence to prove Caronna innocent. What if you find something to prove him guilty?"

"My firm," I said carefully, "only represents clients who are innocent. Naturally, we take the stand that they are innocent until proved guilty, but we will not conceal evidence if we believe it would clear anyone else. If we become convinced of a client's guilt, we drop out of the case. However, a good deal of leeway is left to the operative on the case. Naturally, we aren't here to convict our clients."

"I see." Loftus was stirring that one around in his mind.

"Mind if I look around?"

"Not at all." He took his feet down from the desk and got up. "In fact, I'll go along. Johnny might not let you by unless I was with you."

*   *   *

When we started up the trail it took me only a few minutes to understand that unless Johnny Holben was deaf as a post it would be impossible to get past his cabin without his knowledge. The trail was narrow, just two good steps from his door, and was of loose gravel.

Holben came to the door when we came alongside. He was a tall, lean old man with a lantern jaw and a handlebar mustache that would have been a dead ringer for the sheriff's except for being less tidy and more yellowed.

"Howdy, Loftus. Who's the dude with you?"

"Detective. Caronna hired him to investigate the murder."

"Huh! If Caronna hired him he's likely a thief himself." Holben stepped back inside and slammed the door.

Loftus chuckled. "Almost as bad as Old Bitner. Wouldn't think that old side-winder was worth a cool half-million, would you. No? I guessed not. He is, though. Bitner was worth half again that much. That niece of his will get a nice piece of money."

"Was she the only relative?"

"Matter of fact, no. There's a nephew around somewheres. Big game hunter, importer of animals, an' such as that. Hunts them for shows, I hear."

"Heard from him?"

"Not yet. He's out on the road with a show of some kind. We wired their New York headquarters."

"Wouldn't be a bad idea to check and see where his show is playing. It might not be far away."

Loftus glanced at me. "Hadn't thought of that. Reckon I'm gettin' old. I'll do that tonight."

"Does the girl get all the money? Or does he get some?"

"Don't know. The Bitner girl, she thinks she gets it. Says her uncle told her she would inherit everything. Seems like he has no use for that nephew. So far we haven't seen the will, but we'll have it open tomorrow."

The path led along the flat top of the mesa over the sparse grass and through the scattered juniper for almost a half-mile. Then we saw the house.

It was built on the edge of the cliff. One side of the house was almost flush with the edge, and the back looked out over a natural rock basin that probably held water during the winter or fall, when it rained.

It was a three-room stone house, very carefully built and surprisingly neat. There were a few books and magazines lying about, but everything else seemed to have its place and to be kept there. There was a dark stain on the table top that identified itself for me, and some more of the same on the floor under the chair legs. Looking at the dishes, I figured that Bitner was alone and about to begin eating when death had struck.

The one door into the house opened from a screened-in porch to the room where he had been sitting. Remembering how the spring on the door had screamed protestingly when we opened it, there was small chance that anyone could have entered unannounced.

Moreoever, a man seated at the table could look out that door and down the path almost half way to Ranagat.

The windows offered little more. There were three in the main room of the house, and two of those opened over that rock basin and were at least fifteen feet above the ground. Nobody could have entered quietly from that direction. The third window appeared to be an even less probable entrance.

It opened on the side of the house that stood on the cliff edge. Outside that window and about four feet below the sill was a cracked ledge about two feet wide, but the ledge dwindled away toward the back of the house so it was impossible to gain access to it from there. At the front, the porch ran right to the lip of the precipice, cutting off any approach to the ledge from that direction.

Craning my neck, I could see that it was fifty or sixty feet down an impossible precipice, and then a good two hundred feet that was almost as steep, but could be scaled by a daring man. The last sixty feet, though, made the way entirely impracticable.

The crack that crossed the ledge was three to four inches wide and about nine or ten inches deep. In the sand on the edge of a split in the rock was a track resembling that of a large gila monster, an idea that gave me no comfort. I was speculating on that when Jerry Loftus called me.

CHAPTER TWO

Night Walker

At the door I was confronted by three people. Nobody needed to tell me which was Blacky Caronna, and I had already seen Johnny Holben, but it was the third one that caught me flatfooted with my hands down and my chin wide open.

Karen Bitner was the sort of girl no man could look at and ever be the same afterward. She was slim and lovely in whipcord riding breeches and a green wool shirt that didn't have that shape when she bought it. Her hair was red gold and her eyes a grey-green that shook me to my heels.

Caronna started the show. He looked like a bulldozer in a flannel shirt. "You!" His voice sounded like a hobnailed boot scraping on a concrete floor. "Where have you been? Why didn't you come and look me up? Who's payin' you, anyway?"

"Take it easy. I came up here to investigate a murder. I'm doing it."

Caronna grabbed me by the arm. "Come over here a minute!" He had a build like a heavyweight wrestler and a face that reminded me of Al Capone with a broken nose.

When we were out of earshot of the others, he thrust his face at me and said angrily, "Listen, you! I gave that outfit of yours a grand for a retainer. You're to dig into this thing an' pin it on that dame. She's the guilty one, see? I ain't had a hand in a killin' in—in years."

"Let's get this one thing straight right now," I said. "I didn't come up here to frame anybody. You haven't got money enough for that. You hired an investigator, and I'm him. I'll dig up all I can on this case and if you're in the clear you'll have nothing to worry about."

His little eyes glittered. "You think I'd hire you if I was guilty? Hell, I'd get me a mouthpiece. I think the babe did it. She stands to get the old boy's dough, so why not? He'd had it long

21

enough, anyway. Just my luck the old billygoat would jump me before he gets knocked off. It's inconvenient, that's what it is!"

"What was your trouble with him?"

He looked up at me and his black eyes went flat and deadly. "That's my business! I ain't askin' you to investigate *me*. It's that babe's scalp we want. Now get busy "

"Look," I said patiently. "I've got to have more. I've got to know something to work on. I don't give a damn what your beef was, just so you didn't kill him."

"I didn't," he said. He hauled a roll from his pocket and peeled off several of the outer flaps, all of them showing a portrait of Benjamin Franklin. "Stick these in your kick. A guy can't work without dough. If you need more, come to me. I can't stand no rap, get me? I can't even stand no trial."

"That's plain enough," I told him, "and it answers a couple of questions I had. Now, one thing more. Did you actually stop before you got to the house? If I knew whether the old man was alive or dead at that hour, I'd know something."

A kind of tough humor flickered in his eyes. "You're the dick, you figure that one out. On'y remember: I didn't stick no shiv in the old guy. Hell, why should I? I could have squeezed him like a grape. Anyway, that wouldn't have been smart, would it? Me, I don't lose my head. I don't kill guys for fun."

That I could believe. His story sounded right to me. He could arrange a killing much more conveniently than this one had happened, and when he would not have been involved. Mr. Blacky Caronna, unless I was greatly mistaken, was an alumnus of the old Chicago School for Genteel Elimination. In any rubout job he did he would have a safe and sane alibi.

Yet one thing I knew. Whether he had killed Bitner or not, and I doubted it, he was a dangerous man. A very dangerous man. Also, he was sweating blood over this. He was a very worried man.

Loftus was talking to Holben, and Karen Bitner stood off to one side, so I walked over to her. The look in her eyes was scarcely more friendly than Caronna's. "How do you do?" I said. "My name is—"

"I'm not in the least interested in your name!" she said. "I know all about you, and that's quite enough. You're a private detective brought up here to prove me guilty of murder. I think that establishes our relationship clearly enough. Now if you have any questions to ask, ask them."

"I like that perfume you're wearing. Gardenia, isn't it? By Chanel?"

The look she gave me would have curdled a jug of Arkansas corn. "What is that supposed to be—the psychological approach? Am I supposed to be flattered, disarmed, or should I swoon?"

"Just comment. How long has it been since you've seen your uncle? I mean, before this trip?"

"I had never seen my uncle before," she said.

"You have a brother or cousin? I heard there was a nephew?"

"A cousin. His name is Richard Henry Castro. He is traveling with the Greater American Shows. He is thirty-nine years old and rugged enough to give you the slapping around you deserve."

That made me grin, but I straightened my face. "Thanks. At least you're concise. I wish everyone would give their information as clearly. Did you murder your uncle?"

She turned icy eyes on me. Just like the sea off Labrador. "No, I did not. I didn't know him well enough to either murder him or love him. He was my only relative aside from Dick Castro, so I came west to see him.

"I almost never," she added, "murder people on short acquaintance—unless they're detectives."

"You knew you were to inherit his estate?"

"Yes. He told me so three years ago, in a letter. He told me so again on Saturday."

"I see. What's your profession?"

"I'm a secretary."

"You ever let anybody in to see your boss?" I asked. "No, don't answer that. How many times did you visit your uncle on this visit?"

"Three times, actually. I came to see him on the day I arrived and stayed approximately two hours. I went to see him the following day, and then the night he was killed."

"How did he impress you?"

She glanced at me quickly. "As a very lonely and tired old man. I thought he was sweet."

*   *   *

That stopped me for a minute. Was she trying to impress me? No. I decided, this girl wouldn't try to impress anyone. She was what she was, for better or worse. Also, with a figure like that she would never have felt it necessary to impress anyone.

For almost an hour we stood there, and I asked the questions and she shot back the answers. She had met her cousin, a big, handsome man given to many trips into the jungle after his strange animals, up to a few years before. He had his own show traveling as a special exhibit with a larger show. They made expositions and state fairs, and followed a route across country, occasionally playing carnival dates or conventions.

Her short relationship with her uncle had been friendly. She had cooked lunch the day before he was killed, and he had been alive when she had left him on her last visit. He had said nothing to her about his trouble with Caronna, but she knew he was very angry about something. Also, he kept a pistol handy.

"He did? Where is it?"

"In the sideboard, on the shelf with some dishes. He kept a folded towel over it, but it was freshly oiled and cleaned. I saw it when getting some cups."

Then Bitner had been expecting trouble. From Caronna? Or was it someone else, someone of whom we had not learned?

That night, in the café, I sat at my table and ran over what little I knew. Certainly, the day had given me nothing. Yet in a sense it had not been entirely wasted. The three suspects were now known to me, and I had visited the scene.

The waitress who came up to my table to get my order was a sultry-looking brunette with a figure that needed no emphasis. She took my order, and my eyes followed her back toward the kitchen. Then I saw something else. She had been reading a copy of *Billboard*, the show business magazine. It was spread out on the counter now.

Bitner's nephew, Castro, was in show business. It was something to think about.

Caronna came in. He was still wearing the wool shirt that stretched tight over his powerful chest and shoulders, and a pair of tweed trousers. He dropped into the chair across from me and leaned his heavy forearms on the table. "You got anything?" he said. "Have you got anything on that broad?"

I cut a piece of steak, then looked up at him. "A couple of things. I'm working on them."

He was in a pleasanter mood tonight, and I noticed his eyes straying around, looking for somebody, something. I even had an idea who he was looking for. "They got nothing on me," he said, not looking at me. "The old man an' me, we had a fuss, all right. They know that, an' that I went up the trail to see him. That wasn't smart of me. It was a sucker's trick, but despite that they've got less on me than on that Bitner babe.

"Nobody can prove I went in the house or even went near it. Holben can testify that I wasn't gone long. Your job is to dig up something that will definitely put me in the clear."

"Maybe I've got something."

He leaned back in his chair, looking me over. It was the first time he'd taken a good look. This Caronna was nobody's fool. He had more up his sleeve than a lot of muscle, but I couldn't see him killing Jack Bitner. Not that way.

Murder was not new to Caronna, but he knew enough about it so he would have had an out. He was in this, up to his neck. That much I believed, and I was sure there was more behind the killing than there seemed. That was when I began to get the idea that Caronna had a hunch who had done the job, and somehow figured to cash in.

The waitress came over, and while I couldn't see their expressions, and she only said, "Anything for you, Mr. Caronna?" I had a hunch they were telling each other a thing or two. She dropped her napkin then, and Caronna picked it up for her. Where did they think I was born? I caught the corner of the paper in my glance as they both stooped, but the paper was palmed very neatly by Caronna as he returned the napkin to the waitress.

Caronna left after drinking a cup of coffee and rambling on a little. When I went over to pay my check, the *Billboard* was still lying there. Deliberately, although I had the change, I sprung one of Caronna's C-notes on her. I was praying she would have to go to the kitchen for change, and she did.

The gave me a chance at the *Billboard* and I glanced down. It was right there in front of me, big as life.

GREATER AMERICAN PLAYING
TO BIG CROWDS IN NEVADA

When I got my change I walked outside. The night was still and the stars were out. Up at the mine I could hear the pound of the compressor, an ever-present sound wherever mines are working.

I really had my fingers on something now, I thought. If Greater American was playing Nevada, then Castro might have been within only a few miles of Ranagat when Bitner was killed.

If Loftus knew that, he was fooling me, and somehow I couldn't picture that sheriff, smart as he was in his own line, knowing about *Billboard*. There was a telephone booth in the hotel, so I hurried over, and when I got the boss in Los Angeles, I talked for twenty minutes. It would take the home office only a short time to get the information I wanted, and in the meantime I had an idea.

Oh, yes. I was going to check Karen Bitner, all right. I was also going to check Johnny Holben. But all my mind was pointing the other way now.

There were several things I had to find out.

Where had Richard Henry Castro been on the night of the murder at the hour of the crime?

What was the trouble between Caronna and old Jack Bitner?

What was the connection between that walking hothouse plant in the café and Caronna? Or between her and Castro? Or—this was a sudden thought—*both* of them?

Had either Holben or Karen seen anything they weren't telling?

It made a lot to do, but the ball was rolling, and in the meantime I had a few definite things to work on. From the sign, I saw that the restaurant closed at ten o'clock, so I strolled back again to the hotel and dropped into one of the black leather chairs in the lobby and began to think.

Not more than a hour after my call went in, I got the first part of an answer. The telephone rang, and it was Los Angeles calling me. The Great American, said the boss, had played Las Vegas the day before the murder . . . and its next date had been Ogden, Utah!

In a rack near the desk were some timetables, and some maps put out by filling stations. I picked up one of the latter and glanced over the map. Something clicked in me. I was hot. It was rolling my way, for there was one highway they *could* have followed, and probably did follow that would have carried them by *not over a mile from the mesa!*

Studying it, I knew I didn't have such a lot, although this did bring another suspect into the picture, and a good hot one. One thing I wanted to know now was the trouble between Caronna and Bitner. I walked restlessly up and down the lobby, racking my brain, and only one angle promised anything at all. Loftus had hinted that Caronna was buying highgrade ore from miners who had smuggled it out of the mines.

Then I looked up and saw Karen Bitner coming down down the stairs from her room.

Somehow, the idea of her staying here had never occurred to me, but when I thought about it, where else in this town could she stay?

Our eyes met, and she started to turn away, but I crossed over to her. "Look," I said, "this isn't much of a town, and it's pretty quiet. Why don't we go have some coffee or something? Then we can talk. I don't know about you, but I'm lonely."

That drew a half smile. After a momentary hesitation, she nodded. "All right, why not?"

Over coffee our eyes met and she smiled a little. "Have you decided that I'm a murderer yet?"

"Look," I said, "you want your uncle's murderer found, don't you? Then why not forget the hostility and help me? After all, I'm just a poor boy trying to get along, and if you aren't guilty, you've nothing to fret about."

"Aren't you here to prove me guilty?"

"No. Definitely no. I was retained by Caronna to prove him innocent. Surprising as it may seem, I think he is. I believe the man has killed a dozen men, more or less, but this isn't his kind of job. He doesn't get mad and do things. When he kills it's always for a good enough reason, and with himself in the clear.

"Also, from what he has said, I have an idea that he wants anything but publicity right now. Just why, I don't know, but it will bear some looking over."

"Do you think old Mr. Holben did it?"

That brought me up short. After thinking it over, I shook my head. "If you want my angle, I don't think those old reptiles disliked each other anywhere near as much as they made it seem. I've seen old men like that before. They had some little fuss, but it probably wore itself out long ago, only neither one would want the other to know. Actually, that fuss was probably keeping both of them alive."

"Then," Karen said, "with both Caronna and Holben eliminated, that leaves only myself. Do you think I did it?"

"I doubt it," I said. "I really do. If you were going to kill a man you'd do it with words."

She smiled. "Then who?"

"That, my dear, is the sixty-four-dollar questions."

She smiled, and then she asked softly, "Who is the Siren of Ranagat? An old flame of yours? Or a new one you've just fanned into being? She scarcely takes her eyes off you."

"My idea is that the lady is thinking less of romance and more of finance. Somewhere in this tangled web somebody started she is weaving her own strands, and I don't think my masculine beauty has anything to do with it."

Karen studied me thoughtfully. "You do all right, at that. Just remember that this is a small town, and you'd be a break here. Any stranger would be."

"Uh-huh, and she has a lot of fancy and obvious eqiupment, but somehow I doubt if the thought has entered her mind. I've some ideas about her."

It was cool outside, a welcome coolness after the heat of the day. The road wound past the hotel and up the hill, and we walked along, not thinking much about the direction we were taking until we were standing on the ridge with the town below us. Beyond, on the other mountain, stretched the chain of lights where the mine stood, and the track out to the end of the dump.

The moon was high, and the mining town lay in the cupped hand of the hills like a cluster of black seeds. To the left and near us lay the sprawling, California-style ranch house where Blacky Caronna lived and made his headquarters. Beyond that, across a ravine and a half-mile further along the hill, lay the gallows frame and gathered buildings of the Bitner Gold Mine, and beyond it, the mill.

On our right, also above and a little away from the town, loomed the black bulk of the mesa. There were few lights anywhere, but with the moon they weren't needed. For a few minutes we stood quiet, our thoughts caught up and carried away by the quiet and the beauty, a quiet broken only by the steady pound of the mine's compressor.

Then, from the shadows behind the buildings along the town's one business street, a dark figure moved. Whether I saw it first, or whether Karen saw it first, I don't know. Her hand caught my wrist suddenly, and we stood there, staring down into the darkness.

It struck me as strange that we should have been excited by that movement. There were many people in the town, most of them still awake, and any one of them might be out and around. Or was there something surreptitious about this figure that gave us an instinctive warning?

I glanced at my watch. By the luminous dial I could see that it was ten minutes after ten. At once, as though standing beside her in the darkness, I knew who was walking down there, and I had a hunch where she was going.

The figure vanished into deep shadows, and I turned to Karen. "You'd better go back to the hotel," I told her. "I know this is a lousy way to treat a girl, but I've some business coming up."

She looked at me thoughtfully. "You mean . . . about the murder?"

"Uh-huh. I think our Cleopatra of the café is about to make a call, and the purpose of that call and what is going to be said interest me. You go back to the hotel, and I'll see you in the morning."

"I will not. I'm coming with you."

Whatever was done now would have to be done fast, and did you ever try to argue with a woman and settle any point in a hurry? So she came along.

We had to hurry, for we had farther to go than our waitress, and a ravine to enter and climb out of, and much as I disliked the idea of a woman coming with me into such a situation, I had to hand it to Karen Bitner. She kept right up with me and didn't do any worrying about torn hose or what she might look like when it was over.

This Caronna was no dope. Stopped flatfooted by the hedge around his place, I found myself respecting him even more. This was one hedge no man would go through, or climb over, either. For the hedge was of giant suhuaro cactus, and between the suhuaro trunks were clumps of ocotillo, making a barrier that not even a rattlesnake would attempt. Yet even as we reached it, we heard footsteps on the path from town, and then the jangle of a bell as the front gate opened.

That would be the girl from the café. It also meant that no entry cound be gained by the front gate. Avoiding it, I walked around to the rear. There was a gate there too, but I had no desire to try it, being sure it would be wired like the front gate.

Then we got a break. There was a window open in the garage. Crawling in, I lifted Karen in after me, and then we walked out the open door and moved like a couple of shadows to the wall of the house. I didn't need to be told that both of us were right behind the eight-ball, if caught.

Blacky Caronna wouldn't appeal to the law if he caught us. Knowing the man, I was sure he would have his own ways of dealing with the situation.

CHAPTER THREE

Until Midnight

Caronna was seated in a huge armchair in a large living room hung with choice Navajo rugs. With his legs crossed, his great shoulders covering the back of the chair, he looked unbelievably huge. He was glaring up at the girl.

Taking a chance, I tried lifting the window. Everything here seemed in excellent shape, so I hoped it would make no sound. I was lucky. Caronna's voice came clearly. "Haven't I told you not to come up here unless I send for you? That damn cowtown sheriff is too smart, Toni. You've got to stay away."

"But I had to come, Blacky. I had to! It was that detective, the one you hired. I saw him looking at my copy of *Billboard*."

"You had that where he could see it?" Caronna lunged to his feet, his face a mask of fury. "What kind of brains you got, anyway?" he snarled, thrusting his face at her. "Even that dope of a dick will get an idea if you throw it at him. Here we stand a chance to clean up a million bucks, and you pull a stunt like that! If he ever gets wise, we're through!"

"But they've nothing on you, Blacky," she protested. "Nothing at all."

"Not yet, they ain't, but if you think I'm letting anybody stand in my way on account of that sort of dough, you're wrong, see? This stuff I've been pickin' up is penny-ante stuff. A million bucks an' I'm set for life. What do you think I brought you up here for? To make a mess of the whole works?

"The way it stands, nobody knows a thing but me. Loftus don't know what the score is, an' neither does this dick, an' they ain't got a chance of finding out unless you throw it in their faces. Let this thing quiet down, an' that dough go where it's gonna' to go, an' we're set."

"You'd better watch your step," Toni protested. "You know what Leader said about him."

"Leader's a pantywaist. All he can do is handle that pen, but he can do that, I'll give him that much. I'll handle this deal, an' if that baby ever wants to play rough, I'll give him a chance."

"You shouldn't have hired that detective," Toni said worriedly. "He bothers me."

"He don't bother me any." Caronna's voice was flat. "Who would think the guy would pull this truth-and-honor stuff on me? It looked like a good play. It would cover me an' at the same time cinch the job on that dame, which was the right way to have it. Then he won't go for a payoff. It don't make no difference, though. He's dumb. He ain't smart enough to find his way out of a one-way street."

There was a subdued snicker behind me, and I turned my head and put a hand over her mouth. It struck me afterward that it was a silly thing to do. If a man wants a girl to stop laughing or talking it is always better to kiss her. Which, I thought, was not a bad idea under any circumstances.

"Now, listen." Caronna stopped in front of her with his finger pointed at her. "You go back downtown an' stay there until I send for you. Keep your ears open. That café is the best listening post in town. You tell me what you hear an' all you hear just like you have been. Keep an eye on Loftus, and on that dick. Also, you listen for any rumble from Johnny Holben."

"That old guy? You really are getting scary, Blacky."

"Scary nothing!" he snapped. "You listen to me, babe, an' you won't stub any toes. That old blister is smart. He's been nosin' around some, an' he worries me more than the sheriff. If he should get an idea we had anything to do with that, he might start shootin'. It's all right to be big and rough, but Holben is no bargain for anybody. He'll shoot first and talk after!"

She turned to the door, and he walked with her, a hand on her elbow. At the door they stopped, and from the nearness of their shadows I deduced the business session was over. This looked purely social. It was time for us to leave.

Surprisingly, we got out without any excitement. It all looked pretty and sweet. We had heard something, enough to prove that my first guess was probably right, and it didn't seem there was any chance of Caronna ever knowing we had visited him.

That was a wrong guess, a very wrong guess, but we didn't know at the time.

We didn't know that Karen's shoe left a distinct print in the grease spilled on the tool bench inside that garage window. We didn't know that she left two tracks on the garden walk, or that some of the grease rubbed off on a stone under Blacky Caronna's window.

In the morning I sat over my coffee for a long time. No matter how I sized the case up, it all came back to the same thing. Caronna hadn't killed Old Man Bitner, but he knew who had. And despite the fact that he wasn't the killer, he was in this up to his ears and definitely to be reckoned with.

That copy of *Billboard* was the tipoff. And it meant that I had to get out of here and locate the Greater American Shows, so I could have a look at Dick Castro. Richard Henry Castro, showman and importer of animals.

Caronna came into the cafe and he walked right over and sat

down at the table. I looked up at him. "I can clear you," I said. "I know who the killer was, and you're definitely in the clear. All I need to know now is how he did it."

He dismissed my information with a wave of the hand. His eyes were flat and black. "Here." He peeled off five century notes. "Go on home. You're through."

"What?"

His eyes were like a rattlesnake's. "Get out of town," he snarled. "You been workin' for that babe more than for me. You've been paid—now beat it."

That got me. "Supposing I decide to stay and work on my own?"

"You've got no right unless you're retained," he said. "Anyway, your company won't let you stay without dough. Who's going to pay off in this town? And," he said coldly, "I wouldn't like it."

"That would be tough," I said. "I'm staying."

The smile left his lips. It had never been in his eyes. "I'm giving you until midnight to get out of town," he snarled. Then he shoved back his chair and got up. There was a big miner sitting at the counter, a guy I'd noticed around. When I stopped to think about it, I'd never seen him working.

Caronna stopped alongside of him. "Look," he said, "If you see that dick around here after midnight, beat his ears off. If you need help, get it!"

The miner turned. He had flat cheekbones, and ears back against his skull. He looked at me coldly. "I won't need help," he said.

It was warm in the sunlight, and I stood there a minute. Somehow, the sudden change didn't fit. What had brought about the difference in his feelings between the time he had talked with Toni and now? Shrugging that one off, I turned down the street toward the jail.

Loftus had his heels on the rolltop desk. He smiled at me. "Got anything?" he asked.

"Yeah," I said. "Trouble."

"I don't mind admittin'," Loftus said, "this case has got me stopped. Johnny Holben knows somethin', but he won't talk. That Caronna knows somethin' too. He's been buyin' highgrade, most of it from the Bitner Mine. That was probably what their fuss was about, but that ain't the end of it."

"You're right, it isn't." Briefly, I explained about being fired, and then added, "I don't want to leave this case, Loftus. I think I can break it within forty-eight hours. I think I have all the answers figured out. Whether I do it or not is up to you."

"To me?"

"Yes. I want you to make me a deputy sheriff for the duration of this job."

"Workin' right for me?"

"That's right."

He took his feet off the desk. "Hold up your right hand," he said.

When I was leaving, I turned suddenly to Loftus. "Oh, yes. I'm going out of town for a while. Over to Ogden on the trail of the Greater American Shows."

"There's a car here you can use," he said. "When are you leavin'?"

"About ten minutes after midnight," I said.

Then I explained, and he nodded. "That's Nick Ries, and he's a bad number. You watch your step."

At eleven-thirty I walked to the jail and picked up the keys to the car. Then I drove it out of the garage and parked it in front of the café. It was Saturday night, and the café was open until twelve.

Karen's eyes brightened up when I walked into the cafe. Toni came over to wait on us. Giving her plenty of time to get close enough to hear, I said to Karen, "Got my walking papers today. Caronna fired me."

"He did?" She looked surprised and puzzled. "Why?"

"He thinks I've been spending too much time with you. He also gave me until midnight to get out of town or that," I pointed at Nick Ries at the counter, "gives me a going-over."

She glanced at her watch, then at Ries. "Are—are you going?"

"No," I said loud enough for Ries to hear. "Right now I'm waiting for one minute after twelve. I want to see what the bear-that-walks-like-a-man can do besides look tough."

Ries glanced over at me and turned another page of his newspaper.

We talked softly then, and somehow the things we found to talk about had nothing to do with murder or crime or Caronna; they were the things we might have talked about had we met in Los Angeles or Peoria or Louisville.

She was getting under my skin, and somehow I did not mind in the least.

Suddenly, a shadow loomed over our table. Instinctively, my eyes dropped to my wristwatch. It was one minute past twelve.

Nick Ries was there beside the table, and all I had to do was make a move to get up and he would swing.

It was a four-chair table, and Karen sat across from me. Nick was standing by the chair on my right. I turned a little in my chair and looked up at Nick.

"Here's where you get it," he said.

My left foot had swung over when I turned a little toward him and I put it against the rung of the chair in front of Nick and shoved, hard.

It was just enough to throw him off balance. He staggered back a step, and then I was on my feet. He got set and lunged at me, but that was something I liked. My left forearm went up to catch his right, and then I lifted a right uppercut from my belt that clipped him on the chin. His head jerked back and both feet flew up and he hit the floor in a lump.

Shaking his head, he gave a grunt, then came up and toward me in a diving run. I slapped his head with an open left palm to set him off balance and to measure him, and then broke his nose with another right uppercut.

The punch straightened him up, and I walked in, throwing them with both hands. Left and right to the body, then left and right to the head. He hit the counter with a crash, and I followed him in with another right uppercut that lifted him over the counter. He dropped behind it and hit the floor hard.

Reaching over, I got a lemon pie with my right hand and plastered it in his face, rubbing it well in. Then I straightened up and wiped my hands on a napkin.

Toni stood there staring at me as if I had suddenly pulled a tiger out of my shirt, and when I turned, Jerry Loftus was standing in the door, chuckling.

CHAPTER FOUR

Trouble Stop

Finding Castro's show was no trouble. It was the biggest thing on the midway at the fair, and when I got inside I had to admit the guy had something.

There were animals you didn't see in any zoo, and rarely even in a circus. Of course, he had some of the usual creatures, but he specialized in the strange and unusual. Even before I started looking around for Castro himself, I looked over his show.

A somewhat ungainly looking animal, blackish in color with a few spots of white on his chest and sides, took my interest first. It was a Tasmanian Devil, a carnivorous animal with powerful jaws noted for the destruction of small animals and young sheep. There was also a Malay Civet, an Arctic Fox, a short-tailed mongoose, a Clouded Leopard, a Pangolin or scaly anteater, a Linsang, a Tamarau, a couple of pygmy buffalo, a babirusa, a duckbilled platypus, a half-dozen bandicoots, a dragon lizard from Komodo, all of ten feet long and weighing three hundred pounds, and last, several monitor lizards, less than half the size of the giants from Komodo, India.

I glanced up when a man in a white silk shirt, white riding breeches, and black, highly polished boots came striding along the runway beside the pits in which the animals were kept. On a hunch I put out a hand. "Are you Dick Castro?"

He looked me up and down. "I am, yes. What can I do for you?"

"Have you been informed about your uncle, Jack Bitner?"

His handsome face seemed to tighten a little, and his eyes sharpened as he studied me. Something inside me warned: This man is dangerous. Even as I thought it, I realized that he was a big, perfectly trained man, who could handle himself in any situation. He was also utterly ruthless.

"Yes, I received a forwarded message yesterday. However, I

had already had my attention called to it in the papers. What have you to do with it?"

"Deputy sheriff. I'd like to ask you a few questions."

He turned abruptly. "Bill! Take over here, will you? I'll be back later." He motioned to me. "Come along."

With a snappy, military stride, he led me to the end of the runway and through a flap in a tent to a smaller tent tent adjoining. He waved me to a canvas chair, then looked over his shoulder. "Drink?"

"Sure. Bourbon if you've got it."

He mixed a drink for each of us, then seated himself opposite me. "All right, you've got the ball. Start pitching."

"Where were you last Sunday night?"

"On the road with the show."

"Traveling where?"

"Coming here. We drove all night."

"How often do you have rest stops on such a drive as that?"

"Once every hour for a ten-minute rest stop and to check tires, cages, and equipment." He didn't like the direction my questions were taking, but he was smart enough not to make it obvious. "I read in the papers that you had three likely suspects."

"Yes, we have. Your cousin, Johnny Holben, and—" deliberately I hesitated a little—"Blacky Caronna."

He looked at me over his glass, direct and hard. "I hope you catch the killer. Do you think you will?"

"There isn't a doubt of it." I threw that one right to him. "We'll have him within a few hours."

"You say *him?*"

"It's a manner of speaking." I smiled. "You didn't think we suspected you, did you?"

He shrugged. "Everybody in a case like that can be a suspect. Although I'm in no position to gain by it. The old man hated me and wouldn't leave me the dirtiest shirt he had. He hated my father before me. Although," he added, "even if I could have gained by it, there wouldn't have been any opportunity. I don't dare leave the show and my animals. Some of them require special care."

"That Komodo lizard interested me. They eat meat, don't they?"

He looked up under his eyebrows. "Yes. On Flores and Komodo they are said to catch and kill horses for food. Men, too, I expect, if the man was helpless. They might even get him if he wasn't. They are surprisingly quick, run like a streak for a short distance, and there are native stories of them killing men. Most such stories are considered fantastic and the stories of their ferocity exaggerated. But me, I think them one of the most dangerous of all living creatures." He looked at me again. "I'd hate to fall into that pit with one of them when nobody was around to get me out."

The way he looked at me when he said that sent gooseflesh up my spine.

"Any more questions?"

"Yes. When did you last hear from Blacky Caronna?"

He shifted his seat a little, and I could almost see his mind working behind that suave, handsome face. "What ever gave you the idea I might hear from him? I don't know the man. Wouldn't know him if I saw him."

"Nor Toni, either?"

If his eyes had been cold before, they were ice now. Ice with a flicker of something else in them. "I don't think I know anyone named Toni."

"You should," I said grimly. "She knows you. So does Caronna. And just for your future information, I'd be very, very careful of Caronna. He's a big boy, and he plays mighty rough. Also, unless I'm much mistaken, he served his apprenticeship in a school worse than any of your jungles—the Chicago underworld of the late Capone era."

That was news to him. I had a hunch he had heard from Caronna but that he imagined him to be some small-time, small-town crook.

"You see," I added, "I know a few things. I know that you're set to inherit that dough, and I know that Blacky Caronna knows something that gives him a finger in the pie."

"You know plenty, don't you?" His eyes were ugly and sneering. "This is too tough a game for any small-town copper, so stay out, get me?"

I laughed. "You wrong me, friend. I'm not a small-time cop

I'm a private dick from L.A. whom Caronna brought over to investigate this murder. I learned a good deal and he fired me, and then the sheriff swore me in as a deputy."

He absorbed that and he didn't like it. Actually, I was bluffing. I didn't have one particle of evidence that there was a tie-up between Castro and Caronna, nor did I know that Castro was to inherit. It was all theory, even if fairly substantial theory. However, the hint of my previous connection with Caronna worried him, for it could mean that I knew much more about Caronna's business than I should know.

This was the time to go, and I took it. My drive over had taken some time, and there had been delays. It was already growing late. I got up. "I'll be running along now. I just wanted to see you and learn a few things."

He got up, too. "Well," he said, "I enjoyed the visit. You must come again sometime—when you have some evidence."

"Why sure!" I smiled at him. "You can expect me in a few days." I turned away from him, then glanced back. "You see, when you were in this alone, it looked good, but that Caronna angle is going to do you up. Caronna and Toni. They'd like to cut themselves in on this million or so you'll inherit."

He shrugged, and I turned away. It was not until I had taken two full steps into the deserted and darkened tent that I realized we were alone. While we were talking the last of the crowd had dwindled away, and the show was over.

My footsteps sounded loud on the runway under my feet, but there was a cold chill running up my spine. Castro was behind me, and I could hear the sound of his boots on the boards. Only a few steps farther was the pit in which the huge dragon lizard lay.

The dank, fetid odor that arose from the pit was strong in the close air of the darkened tent with all the flaps down. With every sense in me keyed to the highest pitch, I walked on by the pit and turned down the runway to the exit. He drew alongside me then, and there was a queer look in his eyes. He must have been tempted, all right.

"You think I killed Bitner," he said. He had his feet wide apart and he was staring at me.

Why I said it, I'll never know, but I did. "Yes," I said, "I think you killed him."

There was a sneer in his eyes. "Why, you fool!" he said.
"You damned fool! If I had, you couldn't prove it. You'd only
make a fool of yourself."

That, of course, was the crux of the problem. I had to have
evidence, and I had so little. I knew now how the crime had been
done. This day had provided that information, but I needed
proof, and my best bet was to push him into some foolish action,
into taking some step that would give me further evidence. He
was, as all criminals are, overly egotistical and overly optimistic,
so with the right words I might light a fuse that would start
something.

We had turned away from each other, but I could not resist the
chance, for what it was worth. *"Ati, ati,"* I said, *"sobat bikin
salah!"*

His spine went rigid, and he stopped so suddenly that one foot
was almost in the air. He started to turn, but I was walking on,
and walking fast. I had told him, "Be careful, you have made a
mistake!" in Malayan . . . for the solution to this crime lay in the
Far East.

At the edge of the grounds I stopped to light a cigarette. He
was nowhere in sight, but I noticed a canvasman I had seen
nearby and the man walked up. "How's for a light, mister."

"Sure," I said. "Wasn't this show in Las Vegas a few days
ago?"

"Yeah," he said. "You from there?"

"Been around there a good bit. Have a hard drive over?"

"Not so bad. We stop ever' so often for a rest."

"Who starts you again—Castro? I mean, after a rest stop?"

"Yeah, an' he usually gives us a break once in a while. I
mean, sometimes when we're movin' at night he lets us rest a
while. Got to, or we'd run off the road."

"Stop many times out of Las Vegas? That desert country must
have been quiet enough to sleep."

"We stopped three, maybe four times. Got a good rest out in
the desert. Twice he stopped quite a while. Maybe an hour once,
maybe thirty minutes again. Boy, we needed it!"

Leaving him at a corner, I walked over to my car and got in.
There were several cars parked along the street and in one of
them I saw a cigarette glow. Lovers, I thought. And that took my

mind back to Karen Bitner. A lot of my thinking had been centered around her these last few hours, and little of it had to do with crime.

The car started easily and I swung out on the highway and headed west. It was a long road I had to drive, across a lonely stretch of desert and mountain road with few towns. When I had been driving for about an hour, a car passed me that looked familiar, but there were a girl and man in it. I grinned. Probably the two I'd seen back in town, I thought.

Wheeling the car around a climbing turn, I made the crest and leveled off on a long drive across some rough, broken country. Rounding a curve among some boulders, I saw a car ahead of me and a man bending over a rear wheel. A jack and some tire tools lay on the pavement, and a girl, her coat collar turned up against the cool wind, waved at me to flag me down.

Swinging to the opposite side of the road, I thrust my head out. "Anything I can do?" I asked.

The girl lifted her hand and she held a gun. "Yes," she said, "you can get out."

It was Toni. If the motor had been running, I'd have taken a chance, but I'd killed it when I stopped, believing they needed help. The man was coming toward us now, and with him was still another man who had unloaded from the car. The first was Nick Ries, Caronna's man, but the other I had never seen before. "Yeah," Nick said, "you can get out."

I got out.

My gun was in my hand, and I could have taken a chance on a gun battle, but it was three to one, and they had a flashlight on my face. I'd have been cold turkey in a matter of seconds. With a flirt of my right hand I shoved my gun off my lap and behind the cushion, covering the movement by opening the door with my left. I got out and stood there with my hands up while they frisked me. "No rod," the new man told Nick. "He's clean."

"Okay, get him off the road. We've got work to do."

They pushed me around behind some rocks off the road. I could have been no more than fifty yards from the road when we stopped, but I might as well have been as many miles. Nick stared at me, his eyes hard with enjoyment.

"Looks like it's my turn now. Tough guy, huh? All right, you tell us what we want to know, or we'll give you a chance to show us how tough you are." He waved the gun at me. "Did you see Castro? What did you tell him?"

"Sure I saw him. I told him he was the guy who murdered Bitner. I asked him what Caronna wanted from him, and when Caronna got in touch with him last. It struck me," I added, and this was for Toni's benefit, "that he was a pretty smart joe. I think you guys are backing the wrong horse. Anyway," I continued, "I'm riding with him."

"You?" Toni snapped. "What do you mean?"

"Hell," I said, offhand, "figure it out for yourself. I was ready to do business with Blacky, but he wouldn't offer enough dough. Castro's a gentleman. He'll play ball with you. That's what you guys should be doing, is getting on his side!"

"Shut up!" Nick snapped. Then he sneered, "You know what happens to guys that double-cross Blacky Caronna? I do. An' I don't want any part of it."

"That's if he's alive," I said. "You guys do what I tell you. You go to Castro."

The line I was using wasn't doing me any good with Nick, I could tell, but I wasn't aiming it at him. I was pretty sure that Toni had her own little game, and at she was playing both ends against the middle. If I could convince her I was playing ball with Castro there was a chance she would lend a hand. A mighty slim chance, but I was in no mood or position to bargain with any kind of a chance.

Of one thing I was sure. When they stopped that car they had no idea of ever letting me get away from this place alive. I had to talk fast. "I never expected," I said, flashing a look at Toni, "to find you out here. If we're going to get anything done, it will have to be done in Ranagat."

"Shut up!" Nick snarled.

"Hold it up a minute, Nick," Toni said. "Let the guy talk. Maybe we'll learn something."

"What I was going to say was this. I'm in this for the dough, like you are. Caronna fires me, so I tie on with Loftus, figuring if I stay where the big dough is, I'll latch onto some of it. So what do I find out? That Loftus and some others have a beautiful case built against Blacky. He's got a bad rep, and the owners are figuring on getting rid of him over this highgrade deal. So they have all gone in together—the mine owners, Loftus, Holben, an' all the rest. They are going to swear Caronna right into the death penalty. By the time that case goes to trial Caronna will be framed so tight he can't wiggle a toe.

"Why do you suppose he wanted me up here? Because he knows they're out to get him. Because he's hotter than a firecracker right now and he can't afford to go on trial.

"What I'm getting at is, why tie yourself to a sinking ship? Caronna's through. You guys can go down with him, or you can swing over to Castro and make more money than you ever will from Caronna."

"But," Ries objected, "the will Castro has leaves the money to him, why should he give us a split?"

"He's leery of Caronna. Also," I said, grinning, "I've got my own angle, but I'll need help. I know how Castro killed the old man."

"How?" Ries said shrewdly.

I chuckled. In the last few minutes I'd been lying faster than I ever had in my life, but this I really knew. "Don't ask me how. You guys play ball with me, and I'll play ball with you."

"No," Nick said. "We got orders to bump you, and that's what we do."

"Wait, Nick." Toni waved a hand at him. "I've got an idea. Suppose we take this lug back to town. We can cache him in the basement at the café, and nobody'll know. Then we can study this thing over a little. After all, why should Blacky get all the gravy?"

"How do we know this guy is leveling with us?" Nick said. "He gives us a fast line of chatter, an'—"

"Wait!" Toni turned to me. "If you know Castro, and if you're working that close to him, you know about the will. Tell us."

Cold sweat broke out all over me. Here it was, and if I gave the wrong answer they'd never listen to me again. Hell. I wouldn't have time to talk! I'd be too dead.

Still, I had an idea, if no more. "Hell," I said carelessly, "I don't know what anybody else knows, but I know that Johnny Leader wrote that will, and I know that Castro stashed it away when he killed Bitner.''

"That's what Caronna figured," Toni said. "This guy is right!''

They didn't see me gulp and swallow. It was lucky I had seen that sign over the small concession on the midway, a sign that said, JOHNNY LEADER, WORLD'S GREATEST PENMAN. And I remembered the comments Caronna had made to Toni about Leader. When I'd glimpsed that sign, it had all come back to me.

At last they let me put my hands down, and we started back to the cars. I wasn't out of the woods by a long way, but I had a prayer now. "Toni," Nick said, "you come with me in this mug's car. Peppy can drive ours. We'll head for Ranagat."

It couldn't have worked out better unless Ries had let Toni and me drive in alone. Nick had Toni get behind the wheel and he put me in alongside of her, then he got in behind. That guy wouldn't trust his grandmother. Still, it couldn't have been much better. My .45 was tucked into the crack behind the seat cushion right where I sat.

As we drove, I tried to figure my next play. One thing I knew, I was taking any chance on being tied up in that basement, even if it meant a shoot-out in the street of Ranagat. Then I heard something that cinched it.

"Blacky's figurin' on an out," Nick said to Toni. "He don't know about this frame they're springin' on him. He's all set to bump the babe and make it look like suicide, with a note for her to leave behind, confessin' she killed Bitner."

A match struck behind me as Nick lit a cigarette. "He's got the babe, too. We put the snatch on her tonight after he found them tracks she left."

"Tracks?" I tried to keep my voice casual. My right hand had worked behind me as I half turned away from Toni toward Nick, and I had the gun in my hand, under the skirt of my coat.

"Yeah," Nick chuckled. "She got into his place through the gargage window an' stepped in some grease on a tool bench. She left tracks."

Toni glared sidewise at me. "Weren't you kind of sweet on her?''

"Me?" I shrugged, and glanced at her with a lot of promissory notes in my eyes. "I like a smart dame!"

She took it big. I'm no Clark Gable or anything, but alongside of Caronna I'd look like Galahad beside a gorilla.

CHAPTER FIVE

The Fight

We rolled into the streets of Ranagat at about daybreak, and then I saw the sight that thrilled me more than any I could have seen unless it was Karen herself. It was Jerry Loftus. He was standing in the door of his office, and he saw us roll into town. This was a sheriff's office car, and he would know I wouldn't be letting anyone else drive for fun, not with Nick Ries in the back seat, whom he had seen me bash the night before.

Something made me glance around then, and I saw two things. I saw a grey convertible, the one I had seen standing back of Castro's tent, turning into Caronna's drive, and I saw Nick Ries leaning over on his right elbow, fishing in his left-hand pants pocket for matches.

My own right hand held the gun, and when I saw Ries way over on his elbow, I shoved down with my elbow on the door handle. The door swung open, and at the same instant I grabbed at the wheel with my left.

The car swung and smashed into the curb and then over it. We weren't rolling fast, but I hit the pavement gun in hand and backing up, and saw Loftus coming toward us as Peggy rolled down the hill in the following car. "Get that guy!" I yelled.

Nick was screaming mad. "It's a double-cross! It's a—" His gun swung up, and I let him have it right through the chest, squeezing the two shots off as fast as I could pull the trigger of my gun.

Nick screamed again and his mouth dropped open, and then he spilled out of the car and landed on his face in the dust and dirt of the gutter.

Another shot boomed behind the car, and I knew it was Loftus cutting loose with his six-shooter. He only shot once.

For once Toni had been caught flat-footed. My twist of the wheel and leap from the car had caught her unawares, and now she stared, for one fatal instant, as though struck dumb. Then her face twisted into a grimace of hate and female fury, and she grabbed at her purse. Knowing where her gun was, I went into action a split second sooner and knocked it from her hand. She sprang at me, screaming and clawing, but Loftus and a couple of passing miners pulled her off me.

"Hold her," I said. "She's in it, too."

"Karen Bitner's disappeared," Loftus told me. "Have you seen her?"

"Caronna's got her."

Diving around the sheriff's car, I sprang for the seat of Peppy's convertible, that had been stopped alongside the street. I kicked her wide open and went up the winding road to Caronna's house with all the stops out. Skidding to a halt in front of the gate, I hit the ground on both feet, and this time I wasn't caring if there was a warning signal on the gate or not. I jerked it open, heard the bell clang somewhere in the interior, and then I was inside the gate and running for the steps.

As I went through the gate I heard something crash, and then a scream as of an animal in pain—a hoarse, gasping cry that died away in a sobbing gasp. I took the steps in a bound and went through the door.

Caronna, his eyes blazing, his shirt ripped half off, was standing in the middle of the room, his powerful, trunk-like legs wide spread, his big hands knotted into fists.

In the corner of the room Castro was lying, and I needed only a glance to see that Richard Henry Castro had tackled a different kind of jungle beast, and had come out on the short end. I could surmise what had happened. Castro must have jumped him, and Caronna had torn the man loose and hurled him into that corner and then jumped right in the middle of him with both feet. If Castro wasn't ready for the hospital I never saw a man who was, and unless I was mistaken, he was a candidate for the morgue.

One chair was knocked over, and the broken body of Castro lay on the floor, blood trickling from a corner of his mouth, blood staining the front of his white shirt and slowly turning it to a wide crimson blotch. Yet his eyes were alive as they had never been, and they blazed up to us like those of a trapped and desperate animal brought to its last moment and backing away from the trapper with bared teeth.

Caronna was the thing that centered on my mind and gripped every sense in my being. Somehow, from the first I had known I would fight that man. Perhaps it began when Shanks had told me I wasn't man enough for him. That had rankled.

I stood there looking at Blacky Caronna, a solid block of bone and muscle mounted on a couple of powerful and thick legs, a massive chest and shoulders, and a bull neck that held his blunt, short-haired head thrust forward. He saw me and lunged.

Did I shoot him? Hell, what man who fights with his hands can think of a gun at such a moment? I dropped mine as Caronna lunged for me, and as I dropped it I hooked short and hard with both hands.

My feet were firmly anchored. I was set just right and he was coming in. My left smashed a bit high, slicing a deep cut in his cheekbone, and then my right smacked on his chin. I might as well have hit a wall. He grabbed at my coat, thinking perhaps to jerk it down over my shoulders, but I whipped up a right uppercut that clipped him on the chin, and as all my weight was driving toward him, I jerked my chin down on my chest and butted him in the face, blocking his arms with my elbows.

He grabbed my forearms and hurled me away from him so hard that I hit a chair and it splintered under me. He came in with a rush, ready to give me the boots as he had Castro, but that was an old story for me from lumber camps and waterfronts, and just as he started to jump, I hurled my body at his legs. He tottered and fell over me, kicking out blindly for my face, and one boot grazed my head, but then I rolled over and came up. He was up with me, and we rushed together like a couple of berserk cavemen.

It was wicked, brutal battling. Through a kind of smoky haze in my mind, caused by crashing punches to my head and chin, I drove into him, swinging with both hands, and he met me halfway. It was fist and thumb, gouging, biting, kneeing. Using elbows and shoulders, butting and kicking. It was barroom, backroom, waterfront style, where anything goes and the man who goes down and doesn't get up fast enough is through . . . and he rarely gets up.

Somebody had said that Caronna had once been a puddler in a steel mill, and he had lost none of his strength. A rocklike fist smashed against my chin, bursting a million lights in my brain. A thumb stabbed at my eye in a clinch, and I butted and gouged my way out of it and then clipped him with a right to the chin as he came in. I struck at his throat with my elbow in close, and then grabbing him by the belt, heaved him from the floor and hurled him back on a table. He kicked me in the chest as I came in, and knocked me into the wall.

Castro was staring at us from the floor, and as well as if it had been my own mind, I knew what went on in his. He had seen no jungle beasts fighting as we fought then, for no jungle beast has ever achieved the refinements of cruelty that man has learned to inject into his fighting. A beast fights to win, and men fight and hate while they fight.

My coat and shirt were gone. Blood streaked my body. I could feel a stiffness in the side of my face, and I knew my eye was swelling shut. There was no time to rest, no rounds, no stopping. I stepped in on the balls of my feet and hooked hard to his chin. He blinked and slammed a right at me that I ducked but I caught a sweeping left that rocked me. Weaving to escape his bludgeoning fists, I got in close and whipped both hands to the body, and then a hard right. I forced him back against the desk and jamming my left forearm against his throat, I slammed three right hands into his body before he threw me off and charged at me like a mad bull. I stabbed a left at his face and he took it coming in as though I'd hit him with a feather duster. My right missed and he hit me in the belly with one that knocked every bit of wind out of me.

He hurled me to the floor and jumped for me with both feet, but I jerked up my knees and kicked out hard with both feet. They caught him midway of his jump and put him off balance, and he fell beside me. I rolled over, grabbing at his throat, but he threw a right from where he lay that clipped me, and then I ground the side of his face into the floor by crushing my elbow against his cheek.

We broke free and lunged to our feet, but he caught me with a looping right that staggered me. I backed up, working away from him, fighting to get my breath. My mouth hung open and I was breathing in great gasps, and he came around the wreck of the table, coming for me.

The cut on his cheekbone was wider now and blood trickled from it, staining the whole side of his face and shoulder. His lips were puffed and bloody, and his nose looked out of line.

He came into me then, but I had my wind and I was set. I jabbed with a left and moved away. He pushed on in, bobbing his head to make my left miss, so I shortened it to a hook and stepped in with both hands. They caught him solidly, and he stopped dead in his tracks. I pulled the trigger on my hard one, and his knees crumpled. But he didn't go down. He shook his head and started for me, his eyes glazed. My left hook came over with everything I had on it, and his cheek looked as if somebody had hit it with an axe.

He came on in, and I let go with my Sunday punch. Sunday punch, hell. He took it coming in and scarcely blinked, hurt as he was. For the first time in my life I was scared. I had hit this guy with everything but the desk and he was still coming. He was slower, but he was coming, and his wide face looked as if somebody had worked on it with a meat axe and a curry comb.

My knees were shaky and I knew that no matter how badly he was hurt, I was on my last legs. He came on in, and I threw a right into his stomach. He gasped and his face looked sick, but he came on. He struck at me, but the power was gone from his punches. I set myself and started to throw them. I threw them as if I was punching the heavy bag and the timekeeper had given me the ten-second signal. I must have thrown both hands into the air after he started to fall, but as he came down, with great presence of mind, I jerked my knee into his chin.

Jerry Loftus came into the room as I staggered back, staring down at Caronna. "I could have stopped it," he said, "but I—"

"Why the hell didn't you?" I gasped.

"What? Am I supposed to be off my trail?" He glared at me, but his eyes twinkled at the corners. "Best scrap I ever saw, an' you ask me why I didn't stop it!"

"You'd better get cuffs on that guy," I said, disgusted. "If he gets up again I'm going right out that window!"

We found Karen in another room, tied up in a neat bundle, which, incidentally, she is at any time. When I turned her loose, she kissed me, and while I'd been looking forward to that, for the first time in my life I failed to appreciate a kiss from a pretty woman. Both my lips were split and swollen. She looked at my face with a kind of horror that I could appreciate, having seen Caronna.

Hours later, seated in the cafe over coffee, Johnny Holben and Loftus came in to join us. Holben stared at me. Even with my face washed and patched up, I looked like something found dead in the water.

"All right," Loftus said doubtfully, "this is your show. We've got Caronna no matter how this goes, due to an old killing back east. That's what he was so worried about. Somebody started an investigation of an income-tax evasion and everybody started to talk, and before it was over, three old murders had been accounted for, and one of them was Caronna's.

"However, while we don't know now whether Castro will live or not with that rib through his lung, you say he was the one who killed Bitner."

"That's right," I said. "He did kill him."

"He never came up that trail past my place," Holben said.

"But there isn't any other way up, is there?" Karen asked.

"No, not a one," Loftus said. "In the thirty years since I came west with a herd of cattle to settle in this country, I've been all over that mesa, every inch of it, and there's no trail but the one past Holben's cabin."

"Your word is good enough for me," I said, "but the fact is, Castro did not come by any trail when he murdered old Jack Bitner. How it was done I had no idea until I visited Castro's show. You must remember that he specializes in odd animals, in the strange and the unusual.

"Crime and criminal practices have been a hobby with me for years. In all the reading and traveling I've done, I've collected lots of odd facts about the ways of criminals in our own and a lot of other countries. Usually, methods are very much in pattern. The average criminal, no matter how he may think of himself, is a first-class dope.

"If he had imagination, he wouldn't be a criminal in the first place. When one does encounter the exception, it is usually in the field of murder. Castro was an exception.

"He was a man who spent money and who liked to spend money, and he was getting old enough so that the jungles held no more lure. He wanted money, and he wanted it fast. There was some old family trouble, of no importance to us, that left a decided dislike between Castro and his uncle. He knew he could never inherit in any legitimate way.

"He got his method from India, a place where he had traveled a good deal. When I saw his animals, something clicked into place in my mind, and then something else. I knew then he had scaled the wall under Bitner's window."

"That's a sheer cliff," Loftus protested.

"Sure, and nothing human could climb it without help, but Richard Henry Castro went up that cliff, and he had help."

"You mean, there was somebody in it with him?"

"Nothing human. When I saw his show, I tied it in with a track I saw on the ledge outside Bitner's window. The trouble was that while I knew how it was done, and that his show had been stopped on the highway opposite the mesa, I had no proof. If Castro sat tight, even though I knew how it was done, it was going to be hard to prove.

"One of the great advantages the law has over the criminal is the criminal's mind. He is always afraid of being caught. He can never be sure he hasn't slipped up; he never knows how much you know. My problem was to get Castro worried, and his method was one so foreign to this country that he never dreamed anyone would guess. I had to worry him, so in leaving I made a remark to him in Malayan, telling him that he had made a mistake.

"Once he knew I had been in the Far East, he would be worried. Also, he knew that Caronna had seen him."

"Caronna saw him?" Loftus demanded.

"Yes, that had to be it. That was the wedge he was using to cut himself in on Castro's inheritance."

"How could Castro inherit?"

"There's a man on his show named Johnny Leader, a master penman with a half-dozen convictions for forgery on his record.

He was traveling with that show writing visiting cards for people, scrolls, etc. He drew up a will for Castro, and it was substituted at the time of the killing."

"Get to the point," Holben said irritably. "How did he get up that cliff?"

"This will be hard to believe," I said, "but he had the rope taken up by a lizard!"

"By a *what*?" Holben demanded.

I grinned. "Look," I said, "over in India there are certain thieves and second-story workers who enter houses and high buildings in just that way.

"Castro has two types of monitor lizards over there in his show. The dragon lizards from Komodo are too big and tough for anyone to handle, and nobody wants to. However, the smaller monitor lizards from India, running four to five feet in length, are another story. It is those lizards that the thieves use to gain access to locked houses.

"A rope is tied around the lizard's body, and he climbs the wall, steered by jerks on the rope from below. When he gets over a parapet, in a crevice, or over a window sill, the thief jerks hard on the rope and the lizard braces himself to prevent being pulled over, and they are very strong in the legs. Then the thief goes up the wall, hand over hand, walking right up with his feet against the wall."

"Well, I'll be damned!" Loftus said. "Who would ever think of that?"

"The day you took me up there," I told him. "I noticed a track that reminded me of the track of a gila monster, but much bigger. The idea of what it meant did not occur to me until I saw those monitor lizards of Castro's.

"Now that we know what to look for, we'll probably find scratches on the cliff and tracks at the base."

Karen was looking at me, wide-eyed with respect. "Why, I never realized you knew things like that!"

"In my business," I said, "you have to know a little of everything."

"I'll stick to bank robbers an' rustlers," Loftus said. "Or highgraders."

"You old false alarm!" Holben snorted. "You never arrested a highgrader in your life!"

We were walking out of the door, and somehow we just naturally started up the hill. Dusk was drawing a blanket of darkness over the burnt red ridges, and the western horizon was blushing before the oncoming shadows.

When we were on top of the hill again, looking back over the town, Karen looked up at me. "Are your lips still painful?"

"Not that painful," I said.

THE END

I HATE TO TELL
HIS WIDOW!

CHAPTER ONE

Cop-Killer on the Loose!

Joe Ragan was drinking his ten o'clock coffee when Al Brooks came in and gave him the news. "Ollie's dead," he said quietly. "Ollie Burns. Shot."

Ragan said nothing.

"He was shot twice," Al told him. "Right through the heart. The gun was close enough to leave powder burns on his coat."

Ragan just sat there holding his cup in both hands. It was late and he was tired, and this information left him stunned and unbelieving. Ollie Burns was his oldest friend on the force. Ollie had helped break him in when he first joined up after the war. Ollie had been a good cop, a conscientious man who had a name for thoughtfulness and consideration. He never went in for rough stuff, knowing the tax payers paid his salary, and understanding he was a public servant. He treated people with consideration and not as if they were avowed enemies.

"Where did they find him?" he said at last. "How did it happen?"

"That's the joker—we don't know. He was found on a phoned-in tip, lying in the weeds on the edge of the big vacant area at the end of Dunsmuir. What he was doing out there in the dark is more than I can guess, but the doc figures he'd been dead nearly an hour, maybe a shade less, when we found him." Brooks hesitated. "They think it was a woman. He smelled of perfume, and there was lipstick on his cheek and collar."

"Nuts!" Ragan got up abruptly. "Not Ollie. He was too much in love with his wife. He never stepped out or played around. I knew the guy too well."

"Well," Brooks said, "don't blame me. You could be right. Anyway, it ain't my idea. It's just what Stigler said."

"Where's Mary? Has she been told?" Ragan thought of that

57

first, for thorough as Mark Stigler was, he was scarcely the type to break bad news to anyone.

"Uh-huh, Mark told her. She's home now, and your girl, Angie Faherty, is with her. They were to meet Ollie at the show at nine, and when he didn't show up Mary got worried, so they went home. It seems he was anxious to see this show with Mary, anyway, and they had planned to go together. She called the station when he wasn't at home, and a couple of minutes after she rang off this call came in telling us there was a body lying out there in the dark."

"Who called in?"

"Nobody knows. The guy said he didn't want to get mixed up in anything and hung up."

"Seems odd, anybody seeing that body so soon," Ragan said.

"Nobody ever goes near that place at night, and only recently has anybody been around it by day. They're building an apartment house there now."

Stigler was at his desk when Ragan walked in, and he looked up, unexpected sympathy in his eyes. "I was going to call you," he said, leaning back in his chair. "Do you want this case?"

"You know I do. Ollie was the best friend I had in the world. And you can forget that woman angle. That won't go for Ollie Burns. He was so much in love with Mary that it stuck out all over him, and he wasn't the type to play around. If anything, he was overly conscientious."

"Well, every man to his own view." Stigler tapped with his pencil. "You aren't a Homicide man, Joe, but I'm going to let you loose on this case. It's the first cop killing we've had in over a year, and we want to get the killer, whoever it is. I want this case busted quick, and I want evidence no smart defense lawyer can break or twist. You understand?"

"Will I work with the Squad?" Ragan asked.

Stigler shook his head. "No, you're on your own. You've got a fresh viewpoint, and you knew more about Ollie than any of us. You can get all the help from us you want, and we'll be working on it too, but you go your own way."

Joe Ragan nodded with satisfaction. This was just the way he wanted it, but it was the last thing he had expected from Mark

Stigler. Stigler was a smart Homicide man but a stickler for the rule book, and turning a man loose to work on his own like this was unheard of for him.

"Mark, did Ollie ever say anything to you about the case he was working on? I mean, in his spare time?"

"No, not a word." Stigler tapped with his pencil. "On his own time? I didn't know that ever happened around here. You mean he actually got out on his own time and worked on cases?"

"Sure. He was a guy who hated loose ends or things left around. Ask Mary some time. The guy would put every tool in its place, put every magazine back in the rack, every book on the shelf. It wasn't a phobia or anything, just that he liked to see things neat. And I know he's had some bug in his bonnet for months now, but what it was I don't know."

"That's a thought," Stigler agreed. "Maybe he got too close to the right answer for somebody's comfort and they knocked him off." He stoked his pipe, then leaned forward to strike a match. "You're right about him being overly conscientious. I remember that Towne suicide, about a year ago. He was always needling me to see if I had anything new on it. Hell, there wasn't anything new. The deal was open and shut. Alice Towne killed herself and there was no other way it could have happened. But it seems Ollie knew her, and it upset him."

"He was like that." Ragan got up. "What have you got so far?"

"Nothing. We haven't found the gun. Ollie's own gun was still in his holster. He was in civilian clothes as he was off duty and on the way to the show."

"Why didn't he go? I knew about that because my girl was going with them."

"Somebody called him just before eight o'clock. He answered the phone himself and Mary heard him say 'Where?' and then a moment later he said, 'Right away.' Then he hung up and turned around and asked them if they would mind meeting him in front of the show at nine, that he had an appointment that wouldn't keep."

"I see." Ragan rubbed his jaw. "Well, I'll look into it. If you want me for the next hour, I'll be at Ollie's home with Angie and Mary."

"You aren't going to ask her about it now, are you?"

"Yeah. She's a cop's wife, Mark. Anyway, it will be better to get her talking and digging into her memory for some facts than sitting around moping. I know Mary, and she won't be able to sleep. She's the kind of a woman who starts doing something when she fells bad. If I don't talk to her she'll be washing dishes or something."

Angie answered the door when he rang. "Oh, Joe! I'm so glad you came. I just don't know what to do. Mary won't lie down, and she won't rest. And—"

"I know." Ragan patted her on the shoulder. "Forget it, honey. Mary's like that. We'll have some coffee and talk to her."

Walking through the apartment he thought about what Stigler had said. Lipstick and perfume. . . . But that didn't sound like Ollie. That was where Stigler was wrong. He hadn't known Ollie as Ragan had. Ollie had never been a chaser. If there had been lipstick and perfume on him when he was found, it had probably been put on him to throw the cops off.

And that call. That was odd, in itself. It might be that somebody had *wanted* the body found, and right away. But why? The man on the phone might have been the killer or somebody working with him. If not, what would a man be doing over in that lot at the time of night? For that matter, what was Ollie doing there? It was a dark, gloomy place scattered with old lumber and bricks among the rank growth of weeds and grass. And right in the middle of town.

"On that call, Angie. Did Ollie say anything? Give you any idea of what it was all about?"

"No, Joe. He seemed very excited and pleased, that was all. He told us it wouldn't take long, but just to be sure, to give him until nine. We went to dinner and then to the theater, but he didn't come. He drove away in his own car. Mary and I went in yours."

At a step in the hall Ragan looked up and his eyes softened. He had known Mary Burns even longer than Ollie. In fact, there had been a time when he had liked her very much. However, that was before he had met Angie and before she had met Ollie. After that they had never even had a date together.

She was a dark-eyed, pretty young woman with a round figure and a soft, pleasant face. If anyone in the world was perfectly suited to Ollie Burns, it had been Mary.

"Mary," Ragan said, "this may seem sudden to you, but I want to ask some questions. You know that every minute counts in these things, and I know you'd feel better with your mind occupied than trying to sleep."

"I'd like that, Joe. I really would." Her eyes were red and swollen, but her chin was firm. She sat down across the table from them, and Angie brought in the coffee pot.

"Now, look," Ragan said quietly. "You're probably the only person alive who knew Ollie better than me. He was never one to talk about his work—he just did it—but he had a funny little habit of popping up with odd comments that had to do with it, and they generally gave some idea of what he was thinking. Unless you knew him they might seem utterly idiotic and imcomprehensible."

"I know." She smiled a little and her lips trembled. "He often did that."

"All right, then. Ollie was working on something on his own time. I have a hunch it was some case the rest of us didn't even think about. Remember that Building & Loan robbery? He stewed over that for a month without saying anything to anybody, and then came up with an arrest and all the necessary evidence for conviction. Nobody even knew he was working on the case.

"Well, I think he was working on something else. I think he was so hot on the trail of something that somebody got scared, and I think, somehow, they led him into a trap tonight. We've got to figure out what he was working on."

Mary shook her head. "I don't know what it could be, Joe. He was on a case, I do know that. I can always tell when there's something on his mind—when there *was* something on his mind. He would sit staring over his newspaper for minutes sometimes or walk out in the yard and sort of fiddle around, pulling a weed here and there. He never liked to leave anything until it was finished, but what it was this time, I don't know."

"Think, Mary! Think back over the past weeks, just anything, any of those absent-minded little remarks he was making. One of them might give us just the lead we want."

She furrowed her brow, and Angie filled their cups again. She looked up doubtfully. "There was something, Joe, just this morning, but it doesn't tell us a thing. He just looked up while he was drinking his coffee and said, 'Honey, there's just two crimes worse than murder.' "

"Nothing more?"

"That was all. He was stewing about something, and you know how he was at times like that. I understood and left him alone."

"Two crimes worse than murder?" Ragan ran his fingers through his dark, curly hair. "I know what one was, I'm sure. He's said it often enough. He thought narcotic peddling was the lowest crime on earth, and I agreed with him. It's a foul racket. I wonder if that was it?"

"What could the other crime be?" Angie asked.

He shook his head, scowling. Slowly, carefully, he led Mary over the past days, searching for some clue, but it was not forthcoming. However, one more thing had turned up. A week before, she had asked him to meet her and go shopping, and he said all right, that he was in the Upshaw Building and would meet her on the corner by the drugstore.

"The Upshaw Building?" Ragan shook his head. "I don't know anything about it. Well," he got up, "I'm going to have to adopt Ollie's methods, Mary, and start doing leg work and asking questions. But believe me—I'm not leaving this case until it's solved!"

Al Brooks was drinking coffee when Ragan walked into the café the next morning. He dropped on the stool beside the vice squad man and ordered coffee.

Al was a tall, wide-shouldered man with a sallow face. He had an excellent record with the force. He grinned at Ragan, but there was a question in his eyes. "I hear Stigler has you on the Burns case. What gives?"

"Uh-uh." Ragan didn't feel talkative. His morning coffee with Ollie Burns had been a ritual of long standing, and the ease and comfort of the big man was much to be preferred to the sharp inquisitiveness of Al Brooks.

"Funny, Stigler putting you on that detail. That's strictly Homicide."

Ragan sipped his coffee. "He figured being Ollie's friend I might know something."

After a minute Brooks looked over at him. "Do you?" he asked.

Ragan shrugged. "Not that I can think of. Something may come to me. Ollie had a habit of making off-hand remarks that tied in with his cases, and he was working on something, I know."

"You don't know what it was?"

"No, and neither does Mary, but we'll think of something."

"I still think it was a woman," Brooks said cynically. "You say he never played around. Hell, what guy would pass up a good-looking babe if she was ready? Ollie was human, wasn't he?"

"Sure," Ragan agreed. "But he was also in love with his wife. The guy had ethics. He was as sincere and conscientious as anybody I ever knew."

"Nuts!" Al got up. "Where did that lipstick come from? You mean he cornered some gorilla in that lot and the guy kissed him? Are you kidding?"

"You've got him wrong. Al. You really have. My hunch is that stuff was used for effect, that the killer wanted us to think it was a woman."

Al Brooks stared at him for a minute, then shrugged. "Have it your way, but take a tip from me and be careful. If he was working on something and it was serious enough to call for a killing, the same parties won't hesitate at another. Don't find out too much."

Ragan chuckled. "That doesn't sound like you, Al. There never was a guy on the force stuck his neck out more than you did in pinching Latko."

"That's another thing. I had him bottled up so tight he couldn't wiggle, and none of his friends wanted any part of it. I had too much evidence."

Ragan pushed back over the stool and got to his feet. "What

the hell! We're cops, and that's our job. We have to take that as it comes; only if they tackle me they'll have a shade different problem than with Ollie."

"What do you mean?" Al asked, lighting a cigarette.

"Why, I'm sort of the rough type, Al. I like it the hard way. If they start shooting at me, I'm going to do some shooting myself. If they start slugging, I'll do some of that, too. I like to play rough, and, brother, when it comes to the killer of Ollie Burns, I'm hunting meat!"

Al Brooks waved a hand and walked out. Ragan stared after him. He had never really liked Brooks, but the man was one of the best men on the force. The way he had broken the Latko gang was an example. Aside from a few petty vice squad raids, it had been Brooks' first job, and it had been one of the best pulled all year. Then a few months later he had followed it with the arrest and evidence for the conviction of the society killer, Clyde Bysten.

Stigler saw him in the hall, hesitated for an instant, then motioned him into the office. "Joe, you knew them. How did Ollie get along with his wife?"

Ragan's head came around with a jerk. "Now, listen, Mark. You aren't going to pull that old gag. Why, they were the most loving and affectionate couple I ever knew."

Stigler stared down at the papers on his desk. "Then how do you explain that he was shot with his own gun?"

"Shot with *what?*" Shock riveted Ragan to the floor.

"That's right. Not with his issue pistol, but another gun that he kept at home. It was a .38 Smith & Wesson. We've found the gun, and the ballistics check. The gun is on our records as belonging to Ollie."

"Oh, no!" Ragan stared at Stigler in mingled indignation and confusion. His mind refused to accept what it had heard. "Anyway," he said, "Mary still has an alibi. She was with Angie at dinner. She was with Angie from seven until I left them, long after midnight."

Stigler shook his head. "She wasn't with her all the time. We've checked, Joe, and Mary Burns left Angie Faherty at the table and went to the powder room. She was gone so long that

Angie was afraid she was ill and went to the rest room. Mary wasn't there.''

"Wasn't there?" Ragan dropped into a chair and passed his hand over his face. "I don't get it, Mark. But I'll swear Mary isn't guilty. I don't care whose gun Ollie was shot with."

"What are you trying to do, Joe? Find Ollie's murderer or protect Mary?"

Ragan's face flamed. "Now, listen, Mark. Ollie's the best friend I ever had, but I'm not going to stand by and see his wife stuck for a crime she could no more do than I could. It's absurd. I knew them both too well."

"Maybe that was it." Mark Stigler's face was cold. "Maybe you did know them too well. Maybe that led to the killing."

Ragan stood flatfooted, staring at Stigler, unable to believe he was hearing correctly. He backed up and sat down.

"Mark," he said thickly, "that's the most rotten thing that was ever said to me, but you're no half-baked cop and you're not a rookie. You must have a reason. Now give it to me."

Stigler looked at him carefully. "Joe, understand this. We have almost no evidence to prove this theory. We do have a lot of hearsay. I might also add that I had never dreamed of such a thing until we found that gun in the weeds, and even then I didn't think of you. That didn't come until Hazel Upton."

"Who's she?"

"She's secretary to George Denby, the divorce lawyer."

"Divorce lawyer?" Ragan exclaimed. "You must be going crazy, Mark!"

"Not a bit. Miss Upton told us that Mary Burns had called there to see her boss, that he was out, but that she had told her that she wanted to get a divorce from Ollie Burns."

"Now I know you're crazy!" Ragan said.

"No, we've got a statement from her. We've also got one from a friend of Mary's, a Louella Chasen, who says that Mary had asked her what her divorce had cost, and who her lawyer had been. Also, she had implied there was another man."

Ragan was completely speechless. Even before this array of statements he couldn't believe it. Why, he would have staked his life on it that Ollie and Mary were the happiest married couple he had ever known. He looked up. "But why me? Where do I come in?"

"You were the friend of the family. You called often when Ollie was on duty, didn't you?"

"Well, sure! But that doesn't mean we were anything but friends. Good Lord, man . . ."

CHAPTER TWO

The Visitors

For several minutes Ragan couldn't speak. He knew how a word here and there could begin to build a semblance of guilt. Many times he had told himself to be on guard against assuming too much, and here it was, facing him in his own life.

There was that old affection for Mary Burns. They could bring all that up, and he had known her before Ollie. He knew how a hard-hitting district attorney could make that look, and how he could insinuate so much more than he actually said about his relations with Mary. Ragan could see the whole picture building very carefully around him. And there were two angles he could not get around! Ollie Burns had been shot with his own pistol, and Mary Burns had no alibi. Worse still was the one thing he could not understand or believe—that Mary had actually talked of divorce.

"Mark," he said slowly, "believe me there is something very wrong here. I don't know what it is or where I stand, but I know as well as I am sitting here that Mary never wanted a divorce from Ollie. I was with them too much. And as for Mary and me, that was a childish thing and has been over for a long time.

"I'm in love with Angie, Mark, and ready to marry her tomorrow if she'll have me. She knows that. Somehow or other we've butted into something very ugly."

Stigler's face didn't change. "Keep on with the case, Joe," he said. "If you can find out anything that will help you, go ahead.

I'm afraid Mary is in a bad spot. You can't get around that gun, and you can't get away from those statements.''

"They lied," Ragan said flatly. "They lied and they know they lied."

"For what? What could they gain? Why, Joe, they didn't even know why we wanted the information. Mary Burns was seen coming out of Denby's office, so we made inquiry. Then we got the statement from his secretary. As Denby was out, he knows nothing about it.''

"Who saw her come out of that office?"

Stigler compressed his lips. "I can't say. It was one of our men, and he had a hunch there was something back of it, and as his hunches have paid off, we told him to look into it.''

"Al Brooks?" Ragan demanded. "Was it Al Brooks?"

"Don't start anything, Ragan," Stigler said sharply. "Remember, you're not in the clear yourself. You make trouble with Al and I'll lock you up as a material witness." His face softened. "Damn it, man, I don't want to believe all this, but what else can I do? Who had access to that gun? She and you. Maybe your girl friend, too. There wasn't anybody else."

"Then you've got three suspects," Ragan said grimly. "I wish you luck with them, Stigler."

Nevertheless when he went outside he felt sick and empty. He knew how much could be done with so little. Still, where *had* Mary Burns gone? And what was all this divorce business?

For a moment he thought about climbing into his car and driving out there to find out what was what. Then he decided against it. There was more to do, much more.

He remembered that Mary said Ollie had called her from the Upshaw Building. There was no reason why that should mean anything, yet it was a place to begin, so he turned his car in that direction and soon was leaving it parked near the drugstore where Ollie had met Mary to go shopping.

The Upshaw Building was a third-class office building with a small café on the ground floor and, across the entrance, a barber shop. There was a newsstand in the foyer of the building, and he walked slowly over to it and began to look over the magazines. There was a red-haired girl behind the counter and he smiled at her. He was a big young man with a winning Irish smile, and the girl smiled back. "Is there something I can find for you?" she asked. "Some particular magazine?"

"Give me a package of gum," he said. Then he looked around. "I was sort of watching for a friend of mine. Big guy with a wide face, weighs about two-twenty. Small scar on his jawbone. Do you know him?"

"Him?" The girl smiled, leaning her forearms on the top of the showcase. "Sure. He comes here a lot, although I don't know what for."

"Maybe to see you?" Joe grinned. "I wouldn't blame him, at that."

"He's a nice guy," she said. "Married, though. I saw the ring. He was talking to me about Nebraska."

"Are you from there? I used to work out in a gym in Omaha. I was a fighter for a while."

"You sure don't look it. I mean, you aren't banged up much. You must have been pretty good."

"Fair." Ragan peeled a stick of the gum. So Ollie had been here more than once? And just standing around? "He's friendly, my friend is. Likes to talk."

"Yes, he does. I like him. He's sort of like a big bear."

"All warm and woolly, eh?"

She laughed. "He did talk a lot, but I like it, and he's easy to talk to. He's a good listener." She looked at Ragan again, appraising his shoulders. "What business is he in? He told me he was looking for an office."

"He's a sort of lawyer. Doesn't handle court cases, just works on briefs, and like that." He asked, "Did he find an office? I expect it's pretty hard these days."

"Oh, they're full up here. Of course, there's that office on the fourth floor. He was sort of interested in that one because nobody was around and he thought they might be going to move out. I don't see why anybody wants an office when they never use it."

"Never use it?" Ragan took it carefully. "Seems kind of dumb, paying rent and not using it. That's like buying a car and parking it in a garage. It doesn't make sense."

"It sure don't, and they've had that office for almost a year. I think Mr. Bradford has been in just twice in all that time. Maybe he comes in at night. I know old lady Grimes—she cleans up around here—she says he's been here several times at night. I asked her about the office, thinking maybe I could find out something for your friend, but she said they had a special lock on the door and they have their own cleaning man who comes twice a week."

Joe Ragan was very thoughtful. He steered the subject to the latest movies and songs, then strolled over to the elevator and went up to the fourth floor.

He had no idea what he was looking for, only that Ollie Burns had been here, and Ollie was not a man who wasted his time. Getting off on the fourth floor he walked slowly down the hall and glanced around. Ahead of him he saw an open door, and just opposite from it a closed door with a frosted upper panel. The name on the door was *John J. Bradford, Investments*. There was a mail slot in the door.

As he walked past, Ragan glanced in the open door at a young man who sat at a desk there. He was a short, heavy-set young man with shoulders like a wrestler. He looked up sharply, and there was something so intent about his gaze that Ragan was puzzled by it. He walked on down the hall and went into the office of a *Jacob Keene, Attorney At Law*.

There was no girl in the outer office, but when he entered she walked out to meet him. She was not a day over twenty, with a slim and lovely body in a grey dress that left little to the imagination but much to think about and more than a little to remember. "Yes?"

Ragan grinned. "Now that's the way I like to hear a girl begin a conversation. It saves a lot of trouble, doesn't it? Usually, they only say it at the end of the conversation."

"Oh, they do?" She smiled and looked him over coolly. "Yes, for you I imagine they do." Then her smile vanished. "Now, may I ask your business please?"

"To see Mr. Keene. Is he in?"

"Just a minute." She turned, and her rounded hips lost nothing by the movement. "A gentleman to see you, Mr. Keene."

"Send him in." The voice was crabbed and short.

Joe Ragan stepped by the girl, and she stood there against the door jamb, looking up at him, her lips parted a little, as he passed. Then she stepped out and drew the door shut.

Jacob Keene was a small man who gave the appearance of being hunchbacked, but wasn't. His face was long and grey, his head almost bald, and his eyes were the eyes of a weasel. He took Ragan in with one glance, then motioned to a chair. "Can't get any girls these days that don't spend half their time thinkin' about men," he said testily. "Women aren't like they were in my day." He looked up at Joe, and suddenly the hatchet face broke into an almost engaging smile. "Damn the women of my day! What can I do for you?"

Ragan hesitated, then decided against any subterfuge. "Mr. Keene, I don't think I'm going to fool you, so I'm not going to try. I'm looking for information and I'm willing to pay for it."

"Son"—Keene's eyes twinkled with deviltry—"your last phrase touches a subject that is very close to my heart. Pay! What a beautiful word. Money! Another beautiful word. Money, they say is the root of all evil. All right, let's get to the root of things!"

"As a matter of fact, I don't have much money, but what I wanted will cost you no effort. Shall we say," Ragan drew ten dollars from his pocket book, "a retainer?"

The long and greedy fingers palmed the ten. "And now, this information?"

"I want to know all you know about John J. Bradford and his business."

Keene's little eyes brightened. The light in them was speculative. "Ah?" He hesitated. "Bradford? Well, well."

"Also, I want to know something about the business across the hall, and about the young man at the desk."

Keene nodded. "Notices everything, doesn't he? Most odd, I'd say, unless he's paid to notice. That could be, you know. Well, young man, you have paid me. A paltry sum, but significant, significant.

"Bradford is a man of fifty, I should say, although his walk seems to belie that age. He dresses well, conservative taste. He calls at his office exactly once each month. The cleaning man takes away the mail."

"The mail?" Ragan studied the idea. "The cleaning man takes it away?"

"Exactly. An interesting fact, young man, and one that has engaged my fancy before this. Ah, yes. Money. We all like money, we all want money, and I think our friend down the hall has found an interesting short cut. People come to his door, but they never knock or try to enter—they just slip envelopes through the mail slot."

Keene glanced at the calendar on his desk. "Wednesday. Four should come today, but they will not arrive together. They never arrive together. Three are women, one a man."

He drew a long cigar from a drawer and bit off the end. "Nice place I have here, son. I see everything and everyone that comes or goes in the hallway. See that mirror? I'm out of the way of the door, but I see without being seen. It helps to while away the time. Not much practice these days, but what I get is good."

Keene leaned forward tensely. "Look, young man. Here comes one of the women now."

She was tall, attractive and no longer young. Ragan guessed she was all of fifty. She walked directly to the slot and dropped a letter in, then turned abruptly and walked away. He was tempted to follow her, but on second thought decided to wait and see what happened.

It was twenty minutes before the second woman came. Joe Ragan sat up sharply, for this woman was Mary's friend, Louella Chasen. The woman whom Mary had, according to Stigler, asked about a divorce lawyer. She too, walking abruptly to the door of Bradford's office, dropped an envelope through the slot, then hurried away.

Keene nodded, his small eyes bright and ferretlike. "You see? They never knock, just slide the envelopes through the door and go away. An interesting business Mr. Bradford has, a very interesting business."

Three women and a man, Keene had said. That meant that another woman and a man were due to arrive soon. He would wait. Scowling, Ragan lighted a cigarette and lounged back in his overstuffed chair, one leg over the arm. Keene busied himself over some papers, seeming to have lost interest. Suddenly, however, he spoke without looking up. "Look into the mirror now," he said softly.

Ragan looked, his eyes speculative. The big-shouldered young man had come out into the hallway and was looking around. He threw several sharp glances toward Keene's office and then returned to his own. A few minutes later a tall young man, fair haired and attractive, if somewhat weak looking, dropped an envelope into the slot, then hurried away. It was almost a half-hour after that when Joe Ragan, growing sleepy from his vigil, glanced up to see the last visitor of the day.

She was young and she carried herself well, and Ragan sat up sharply, sensing something vaguely familiar in her walk. Then she turned her head toward Keene's office, and he saw her face. It was Angie Faherty, his own girl friend. She dropped a letter into the slot and turned away.

"Well," Keene said briskly, "you've had ten dollars worth. Those are the four who come today. Three or four will come tomorrow, and so on each day. They bunch up, though, on Saturday and Monday. Can you guess why?"

"Saturday and Monday? Probably because they draw their pay on Saturday. They must be making regular investments."

Keene chuckled. "Investments? Maybe. And that last young lady—she has been coming here longest of them all. Why, it's over six months now since she started coming here with her . . . donations."

Ragan heaved himself erect. "See you later. If anything turns up let me know. Or better, save the information for me. I'll be around."

"With more money," Keene said cheerfully. "With more money, young man. Let's grease the wheels of inflation."

CHAPTER THREE

Man on the Fire Escape

Angie was drinking coffee at their favorite place when Ragan walked in, and she looked up, smiling. "Have a hard day, Joe? You look worried?"

"This case gives me the willies. I'm afraid they're going to make some trouble for Mary."

"For Mary?" Angie was amazed. "How could they?"

He explained swiftly and her eyes darkened with righteous anger. "Why, that's silly! You and Mary! Of all things!"

"I know," he said. "But a district attorney could make it look bad. And where was Mary when she left you, Angie? Where could she have been? That's what gets me."

"We'll ask her. Let's go out there now."

"All right." He got up. "Have you eaten?"

"No, I came right here from home. I didn't stop anywhere."

His eyes found the pigeons on the walk, and he watched them pecking up crumbs thrown from the restaurant. "Been waiting long?"

"Long enough to have eaten if I had thought of it. As it was, all I got was this coffee."

That made the second lie. She hadn't been here for some time. And she hadn't come right here from home. He tried to give her the benefit of the doubt. Maybe the visit to the Upshaw Building was so casual she didn't think about it. Still, it was far out of her way in coming from home to here.

All the way out to Mary's he mulled that over. And another idea kept cropping up in his mind. He was going to have to get into that office of Bradford's. He was going to have a look at those letters and see what they contained. Moreover, there might be another clue.

Yet what did he have to tie them to Ollie's murder? Little enough, actually. No more than the fact that Ollie had loitered in the Upshaw Building, that he had been interested in Bradford's office, and that Louella Chasen had volunteered the information that Mary Burns had asked for a divorce. That was a flimsy tie, yet it intrigued him, and it was a beginning.

Try as he would he could come up with no other clue to the case that Ollie Burns had been working on, unless he went back to the Towne suicide. Mark Stigler had mentioned that as holding Ollie's interest, and it was worth a bet. The first thing tomorrow he would get on that angle.

He remembered Alice Towne. Ollie had known her slightly through an arrest he had made in the neighborhood. She had been a slender, sensitive girl with a shy, sweet face and large eyes, and her sudden suicide had been a blow to Ollie, for Ollie liked people and had considered her a friend.

"You know, Joe," he had said once, "I always felt maybe that was my fault. She started to tell me something once, then got scared and shut up. I should have kept after her until she talked, because I knew something was bothering her. If I'd not been in so much of a hurry, I could probably have figured it out."

Mary opened the door for them and they walked in. Joe sat down with his hat in his hand. "Funeral tomorrow?" he asked gently.

Mary nodded. "Will you and Angie come together?" she asked.

"Why, maybe you'd better have Angie with you," Ragan suggested. "You two stick together. I'll be working right up to the moment, anyway."

Mary turned to him. "Joe, you're working on this case, aren't you? Is there any other way I can help?"

Ragan hated it, but he had to ask. "Mary, where did you go when you left Angie the night Ollie was murdered?"

Her face went stiff and she seemed to have difficulty moving her lips. "You don't think I'm guilty, Joe? You surely don't think I killed Ollie?"

"Of course not!" He gave her that flat and straight. "Not even a little, but they're asking that question, Mary, and they'll want an answer."

"They've already asked, and I've refused to answer," Mary said quietly. "I shall continue to refuse. It was private business, in a way, except that it did concern someone else. I can't tell you, Joe."

Their eyes held for a full minute, and Ragan got up. "Okay, Mary. If you won't, you've got a reason, but don't forget that reason may be a clue. Don't hold anything back. Now let me ask you: Did you ever think of divorce?"

"No." Her eyes looked straight into Ragan's. "If people say I did, they're lying. From what Mr. Stigler said, I believe someone has said that. It simply is not true."

After Ragan left them he thought about that. He was willing enough to take Mary's word for it, knowing her, but would anybody else? In the face of two witnesses who would say the contrary? And the fact that Ollie had been shot with his own gun.

Moreover, he was getting an uneasy feeling. Al Brooks was hungry for fame and advancement. He liked going around and he liked spending money, and despite the fact that he always seemed to have plenty, Ragan knew that a step up in rank would suit him very well indeed. If he could solve the killing of Ollie Burns and pin it on Mary or Ragan, he would not hesitate. He was a smart, shrewd man, and he had connections.

Ragan had several lines of study to follow now. The Towne case was an outside and remote chance, but the Upshaw Building promised better results.

What had Angie been doing there? What did the mysterious letters contain? Who was Bradford?

Taking his car, Ragan drove swiftly across town, heading for the Upshaw Building. He had his own ideas about what he was going to do now, and the law would not condone them. Nevertheless, he was going into that Bradford office or know the reason why. His visit to Keene's office had not been without profit from that angle. He had noticed that the fire escape under Keene's window also extended to what was probably a window of the Bradford office. The lock on the Bradford office was a very good one, placed on it by the tenant, and it would be anything but simple to open.

Parking the car a block away, Ragan walked up the street. Then, taking a quick gander either way, he walked on to the Upshaw Building. There was a night elevator man drowsing over a newspaper, but by walking softly Ragan got to the stairs and went up rapidly. That night man might be in the pay of Bradford. In any event, the less anyone knew of Ragan's activities the better he would like it.

The fourth floor was dark and still. He stood for a moment at the head of the steps, watching and listening. Not a sound broke the stillness. Walking carefully, he went along the hall to the door of Keene's office. He searched for one of his skeleton keys that might open the door. At the same time, automatically he tried the knob. The door opened under his hand. He stepped inside, then froze in his tracks.

The body of a man was slumped over the desk.

He sat in the swivel chair, face against the desk, his arms dangling at his sides. All this Ragan saw in the sporadic flashes from a large electric sign on the roof of the building across the street, and he closed the door softly behind him, studying the shadows of the room.

It was dark and still, the room lighted only by the indefinite glare from that electric sign. The corners were dark, and the shadows lay deep along the walls of the room.

Ragan's gun was in his shoulder holster, and it felt reassuring in its weight. Moving forward, careful to touch nothing, he leaned forward and spoke softly. "Say, you?"

No reply, no movement. With a fountain pen flash, he studied the situation.

Jacob Keene was dead. There was a blotch of blood on his back where a bullet had emerged. There was, Ragan noted as he squatted on his heels, blood on Keene's knees and on the floor under him, but not much. Not enough. He had a hunch then that Jacob Keene's body had been moved. Flipping on the light switch, he glanced quickly around the office to ascertain that it was empty. Then he began a careful survey of the room.

Nothing was disturbed or upset. It was as he had seen it that very afternoon, with the exception that now Keene was dead. Careful not to touch anything, he knelt on the floor and studied the wound. The bullet had apparently entered low in the abdomen and ranged upward, an odd angle. The gun, which he had missed seeing before, lay under Keene's right hand.

Suicide? That seemed to be the idea, but remembering Keene

of that afternoon, Ragan shook his head. Keene was neither in the mood for suicide nor was he the type of man for it. No, this was murder. It was up to Ragan to call Homicide, but he hesitated. He had a few other things to do first.

The first thing was to carry out his original idea to see the inside of that office of Bradford's. To all appearances Keene had been murdered elsewhere and brought here. Maybe he had been killed trying to do exactly the same thing Ragan was about to attempt.

Absolute silence hung over the building. Ragan put his ear to the wall and listened for minutes, waiting for a sound, but there was none. Carefully, then, he eased up the window. Four stories below a car buzzed along the street, then silence. The windows facing him were all blank and dark. Stepping out on the fire escape, a drop of rain struck his face, and he glanced up toward the lowering clouds. If it rained, that would be good, for in a rain no one would be inclined to look up.

With utmost care, flattened against the building, he made his way the few feet to the other window. It was closed and unlighted. After listening, he put his hand out carefully, hoping the window was not locked. It was, though. He took the chewing gum from his mouth and plastered it against the glass near the lock, then tapped it with the muzzle of his gun. The piece could not fall inward as it was against the lock, and he lifted it out very carefully, then slid a finger through and released the lock.

The window slid up and he lowered his feet to the floor of the Bradford office, then moved swiftly away from the window and against the wall. For a long time he stood absolutely still, studying the office. Then, using utmost care, he began a minute examination.

For one hour he shook that office down, but it offered nothing. Nothing? One thing only: a large damp patch on the floor, a patch of dampness where blood might have been washed off. But blood can never be washed away completely in such a hurried job, and Ragan knew what a laboratory test would prove. However, he was not looking now for a solution to the murder of Jacob Keene, but for information that would offer a motive for the killing of Ollie Burns.

The office was like any office except that every clue proved it was little used. There was a typewriter, paper, carbon and second sheets, boxes of envelopes. The blotter on the desk was new, unused. There were paper clips, rubber bands, a dictionary and various other things. The filing cabinets had varied references to mines and industries. The office was all it purported to be, except for that damp place on the floor.

Then he noticed something he had missed. It was a tiny, crumpled bit of paper lying on the floor under the desk as though someone had tossed it to the wastebasket and missed. Retrieving it, Ragan unfolded it carefully and flashed his light upon it.

ME 34556.

Ollie Burns' phone number!

Here was a definite lead, but to where? Irritated, Ragan stood in the center of the office, wondering what to do next. Somewhere near him might be the clue that he needed. Suddenly there came to mind one of the titles of the companies he had noticed in leafing through the files, and swiftly open the drawer labeled *T*. In a moment he had it: Towne Mining & Exploration. Under it was a list of code words and then a list of sums of money indicating that fifty dollars a month had been paid until the first of the year when the payments had been stepped up to one hundred a month. Four months later there was the entry: "Account closed, 20 April."

His heart was pounding now, for Ragan remembered very clearly that the suicide of Alice Towne had been discovered on the 19th of April.

Towne Mining & Exploration Company. . . . Was there such a firm? He had noticed that in each drawer of the cabinet there were several well-known companies listed, but no payments on any of them. These must be a blind—probably for blackmail.

What had Ollie told Mary? *"There are just two crimes worse than murder."* Dope peddling and blackmail.

Who else had come to this office? Louella Chasen. Ragan drew out the drawer with the *C* on its face, thumbed through it to a folder entitled Chasen Shipping.

A quick examination showed the payments here to have progressed from ten dollars a month to a hundred a month over a period of four years.

Louella Chasen was the one who had said she recommended a divorce lawyer to Mary Burns. Would Louella Chasen lie to protect herself? If blackmail would force such sums of money from her would it not force her to perjure herself?

Hazel Upton, the secretary to Denby, the divorce lawyer. Her name, thinly disguised, was here also.

It was the merest sound, no more than a whisper of sound as of cloth brushing paper, that interrupted him. Frozen in place, Ragan listened, heard it again. It came from the office of Jacob Keene, where the murdered attorney still lay.

Ragan's hand went to his gun, a reassuring touch only. This was neither the time nor the place for a gun. Swiftly, his eyes swung to the window. It stood open, and so did the window in the office of Jacob Keene. If someone had come there, that someone would see the open window, and a glance, if that someone leaned out would show this window to be open too. And if the man who was in the next room happened to be the murderer . . .

Even as he thought of that, Ragan knew there was something else in that cabinet that he had to see—the folder on Angie Faherty.

There was no time for that now. The door into the hall was out of the question, for it was locked from the outside with a patent lock. The only exit from this office was the way he had come.

Like a wraith, Ragan slid from the filing cabinet to the shadow near the big safe, then to the blackness of the corner near the window. Even as he reached it, he heard the sound of a shoe touching the iron of the fire escape. The killer was coming in.

It was very still. Outside a whisper of rain was falling now and there was the sound of traffic and the buzz of tires on the wet pavement of the street below. The flashing electric sign did little to light the room, and Ragan stood there, holding his breath and waiting.

A stillness of death hung over the building. The murderer on the fire escape was waiting, too, and listening. Listening for some movement from Ragan.

Did he know Ragan was there? And who was it out there? It was a good question.

With a quick glance at the window, Ragan gauged the distance to the telephone. Then, moving as softly as possible, he glided to the side of the desk and crouched beside it. With his left hand he shifted the phone to the chair. Then he lifted the receiver.

Holding the phone, he waited. Suddenly, tires whined on the pavement, and he dialed Operator, hoping the sound would be covered by the passing car. "Police Department!" he whispered. "Quick!"

In a moment a husky voice answered, "Police Department!"

"Get this the first time," Ragan breathed. "There's a prowler on the fire escape of the Upshaw Building."

Ragan's voice was a low whisper, but the desk sergeant got it all right. He repeated it, and then Ragan eased the phone back on the cradle. The light from the sign flashed, and from his new position he could see the dim outline of the figure on the fire escape edging closer.

The police would be here in a minute. If only the figure on the fire escape would linger until . . . He heard the siren's whining far off, then, and grinned. It was going to be nip and tuck now, fast work whatever happened, and even as the siren whined closer, Ragan heard the man outside give vent to a muffled curse. Then the cars slid into the street below and he heard feet clang on the fire escape, going down.

CHAPTER FOUR

One More Corpse

For a breath-taking instant, Ragan waited, then ducked out the window even as a police spotlight flung its glare up the wall. One flashing instant before the glare had reached him, he ducked into the Keene office. Below, he heard a yell. "There he is!"

They had spotlighted the other man. Ragan ducked out the door, pulled it shut and raced for the back stairs. Down he went, three at a time, risking his neck with every jump. When he hit the main floor he slowed down and saw the watchman standing in the wide door, craning his neck. On cat feet Ragan slipped up behind him, got one foot on the sidewalk, and said, "Did they get him?"

The watchman jumped a foot. He turned around, his face white, and Ragan flashed his badge. "Gosh, mister, you sure scared hell out of me! What's the matter?"

"Prowler reported on the fire escape of this building," Ragan said. "I'm watching this door."

Sergeant Casey came hurrying up. When he saw Ragan he slowed down. Casey was one of Ragan's buddies, for this was a burglary detail if the prowler had been robbing offices. "Hello, Ragan. Didn't know you were here."

"Did you get him?"

"No, we sure didn't, but Brooks almost did."

"Al Brooks?" Ragan's scalp tightened. What had Brooks been doing here? Tailing Ragan? Ragan hadn't even thought of them putting a tail on him, but Brooks was just the guy to do it.

"Yeah, he was on the street and saw somebody up the fire escape. He started up after them just as we came up. Fellow got away, I guess."

"Ain't been nobody around here," the watchman stated flatly. "Only Mr. Bradford, and he left earlier."

"What time was he here?" Ragan asked.

"Maybe eight o'clock. No later than that."

Eight? It was now almost one in the morning, and Keene had not been dead long when Reagan had found him. Certainly no more than an hour, at a rough guess. His body hadn't even been cold.

Al Brooks came around the corner of the building with two patrol car officers. His eyes widened when he saw Ragan, then narrowed. He was suddenly watchful, cagey. "How are you, Joe? Didn't expect to see you here."

"I get around," Ragan said quietly, shaking out a cigarette.

"You'd better get your nose clean before you get around too much," Brooks said.

Casey interrupted them. "We'd better go through the building, Ragan," Casey said. "Now that we're here. The man might be hiding upstairs."

"Good idea," Ragan said. "Let's go!"

Everything was tight and shipshape all the way to Keene's

office. Ragan was letting Casey and a couple of the boys precede him a little. It was his idea to have them find the body. It was Casey who did.

"Hey!" he yelled. "Dead man here!"

Ragan and Brooks came on the run. "Looks like suicide," Brooks commented. "I doubt if this has anything to do with the prowler, although it might."

"Doesn't look like he got in here," Casey said.

"But the window's op—" Brooks stared. The window was closed. "You know," he said, "when I was coming up this fire escape I'd have sworn this window was open."

He turned to the body at the desk. "Looks like suicide," he said. "The gun's right where he dropped it."

"Except that it wasn't!" Ragan said dryly. "This man was stabbed before he was shot."

"What?" Brooks whirled and stared suspiciously. "Where do you get that stuff?"

"Look." Ragan indicated a narrow slit just above the bullet wound in the stomach. "That looks to me like he'd been stabbed; then somebody put the gun barrel on an angle calculated to let the bullet follow the path of the knife. Then a murder becomes an apparent suicide. And I'll bet the gun belongs to Keene."

Brooks' head came up. "How did you know his name?"

"From the door," Ragan said, "Jacob Keene, attorney at law."

Brooks shut up, but Ragan didn't like the look in his eyes. Brooks was getting ready with the knife.

Meanwhile, Ragan did some wondering. What had become of the prowler? Up above somewhere? That was where he wanted to look. He was still thinking about that and carrying on a preliminary examination of the office without disturbing anything when Mark Stigler came in. He looked quickly at Ragan, then at Brooks.

"Lots of talent around," he said grimly. "What is it, murder or suicide?"

The slit in the material of the shirt was barely visible, but Ragan indicated it. "Could be," Stigler agreed doubtfully. "Seems kind of far-fetched, though. Who was this guy?"

"From his files," Ragan said, "he must have been a sort of a ambulance chaser, a shyster, but handling a good many minor criminal cases, too."

Stigler's boys got to work while Stigler stood there chewing on a toothpick and staring around the room. Mark Stigler was a smart cop and a conscientious one. Nor was he any fool. He walked over to the window and glanced at it, then rested his hand on the sill. "This window had been open," he said. "The sill is damp."

"The prowler," Casey said. "Maybe it was him."

Stigler looked around, frowning, and Al Brooks shoved his hat back on his head and took over. Quickly, he explained that he had been on the street below and, glancing up, saw the dark figure outside the window on the third floor. Just as he started up he heard the sirens and the cars showed up. "About that time," he added, "Joe Ragan showed up."

Stigler nodded and glanced at Ragan. "How are you coming on the Burns case?"

"Good enough," Ragan said. "I'll have it busted by the end of the week."

Stigler looked at him thoughtfully. "We've got a strong case against his wife," he said, "and Brooks thinks she killed him. She or somebody close to her."

That meant Ragan, of course.

"Brooks doesn't know what he's talking about," Ragan said. "Mary Burns loved her husband, loved him in a way Brooks couldn't even understand."

Brooks laughed unpleasantly. "Bud," he said grimly, "I hope you're right, but I've piled up a lot of evidence. And there *might* be somebody else in it, and I don't mean Mary Burns!" He was grinning at Ragan when he said it, and Ragan knew he was hinting at Angie.

Ragan walked over to him, fists knotted. "Listen, Brooks," he said, "don't try to pin anything on any friends of mine, see? If you've got the goods, all right. But you start a frame and I'll bust you wide open!"

"Cut it out, Ragan!" Stigler said sharply. "Any more talk like that and you'll draw a suspension. I won't have fighting on a job of mine."

"Anyway," Al Brooks replied softly, "I don't think he could do it."

Ragan just looked at him. Some day, he knew he would take Brooks and take him good. Until then, he could wait.

There was nothing for Ragan to do, so he got out of there. He wanted to be away where he could do some thinking. An idea had occurred to him that was positively insane, and yet . . .

Where had Al come from? How had he happened to be on the scene so quick?

The street below, within sight of the window, had been empty. Yet the searchlights of the police cars had caught the figure, who turned out to be Al Brooks, on the fire escape.

Ragan thought about that. He thought about that and a few other interesting things about Al Brooks. Such as: Al Brooks dressed better than any man on the force. He drove a good car, one of the best made. He lived in good apartments and he always seemed to have money, more money than a police detective should have, maybe.

Now that he was working on the idea, a lot of things occurred to him. He got into his car and started for home, thinking about it. This was something he could get busy on; this was something he could really work over. It had been Al Brooks who first suggested that Mary Burns might have killed her husband.

Stopping the car, Ragan got out and crossed the walk. There was a strange car parked at the curb a few doors away, and he stopped and looked at it thoughtfully. For some reason the car disturbed him, and he turned and walked toward it. There was no one inside, but it was not locked. Opening the door, he looked at the registration card. Valentine Lewis, 2234 Herald Place.

The name meant nothing to him, and he turned away and walked up to his private entrance and fitted the key in the lock. As he opened the door he was thinking that the blackmailer could have influenced both Hazel Upton and Louella Chasen to start the divorce rumor, and if Brooks . . . He stepped into the door and the roof fell on him.

Wildly, grabbing out with both hands, Ragan fell forward to his knees. He couldn't comprehend what was happening. Then there was a smashing blow on his skull as he was hit a second time, and he slid forward, faster and faster, head first down a long slide into darkness.

When Ragan fought his way out of it he was lying on the floor, and his head felt like a balloon. Grey light was filtering into the room, and he decided that it must be almost daylight. For a while he lay still, just trying to gather his thoughts together, and then he got to his hands and knees and to his feet. Swinging over, he dropped on the divan and sat there with his head in his hands.

His skull was drumming as if an insane snare drummer had gotten hold of it, and his mouth felt sticky and full of cotton. He lifted his head and almost blacked out. Slowly he stared around the room. Nothing had been taken that he could see. Then he felt for his handkerchief and realized that his pockets had been turned inside out.

Staggering to the door he peered into the street. The strange car was gone.

"Val Lewis," he told himself grimly, "you'd better have a good story if you aren't guilty, and if you slugged me, God help you!"

Somehow, he got out of his clothes and into a shower, and then tumbled into bed. His head was cut in two places from the blows, but what he wanted most was sleep. It wasn't until well past noon before he awoke, roused by the phone.

It was Angie. "Joe!" Her voice was frightened and anxious. "What's happened to you? Where are you?"

"I must be home," he said. "When the phone rang, I answered it. Where are you?"

"Where am *I*?" Her voice was angry. "Where would I be? Don't you remember our luncheon date?"

"Frankly, I didn't," Ragan said. "I got slugged on the head last night, and—"

"At least," she interrupted, "that's an original idea."

"And true," Ragan said. "I was visiting an office in the Upshaw Building and then—"

Her gasp was audible over the phone. "Joe! Where did you say? The Upshaw Building?"

"That's right." He was remembering her call there. "Some people up there play rough, honey. They murdered a lawyer up there last night. He knew too much and was too curious about a fellow named Bradford.''

She didn't say a thing. Not one thing. ''The slugging,'' Ragan continued, ''happened here, after I got home. I think somebody wanted to find if I carried anything away from that building.''

That was an idea that came to him while he was talking, but it made some kind of sense. What other reason was there? Thinking it over, it struck him as remarkable that he hadn't been killed out of hand. They had probably killed Ollie Burns for little more. Or less.

She still didn't speak, so he asked her. ''How's Mary? Is she all right?''

''Joe!'' She was astonished. ''You don't know? She was arrested this morning. Al Brooks arrested her!''

Brooks. Ragan's grip tightened on the phone until his fist turned white. ''So he arrested her. All right, that does it. I'm going to blow everything loose now.''

''What are you going to do?'' She sounded anxious.

''Do?'' Ragan's voice was rough. ''Honey, that whole case is built on a bunch of lies. I happen to know that Louella Chasen and Hazen Upton were forced to lie by a blackmailer. Right now is where I start trouble.''

''Joe, did you say . . . a blackmailer?''

''Yes, Angie, a blackmailer. The same man who hounded Alice Towne to death and started Ollie Burns hunting for him. The same one who murdered Ollie, and last night murdered Jacob Keene.''

''You mean,'' he could tell nothing from her voice, ''you *know* all that? You can prove it?''

''No,'' Ragan said. ''I can't prove it. But I will, honey, I will!''

After he hung up Ragan got into his clothes and looked at his face. It was an Irish face, slightly altered by a right hook that he'd stopped with his nose long ago. The hook hadn't done so much damage, leaving only a lump, and a small one, on the bridge. What had happened to the guy who put it there was in the record books. He'd lost on a knockout in the fourth round and never fought again.

A razor smoothed the beard from his face while Ragan turned

the case over in his mind. He decided to start with Val Lewis and then work his way through Hazel and Louella. Also, he was going to have to talk with that luscious job Keene had for a secretary, and maybe with the sharp-eyed lad who kept an eye on Bradford's door.

For the next two hours Ragan was a busy man. He skidded around to several people and checked through the files of some back papers at the morgue of the *Times*. Also, he checked on the address Val Lewis had on his steering wheel post.

The door was answered by a dyspeptic-looking blonde in a flowered gown that concealed little. She looked rather the worse for wear and had a shadow of a blackeye.

"I'm looking for Valentine Lewis," Ragan said politely. "Does he live here?"

She looked Ragan over with a fishy eye. "What do you want to see him for?"

"Veteran's Administration," Ragan said vaguely. "Some money for him."

"That's a lousy joke," she said coldly. "Val was in stir all during the war. Come again."

"Police Department." Ragan flashed his badge and pushed by her.

She came to with a yell, strident and furious. "You get out of here, copper! You got no search warrant!"

"Yes, I have," Ragan said, and, taking one from his pocket, flashed it at her. She didn't get a chance to see more than the top of it, for it was just a form he'd partly filled out himself. She didn't ask any questions but stood by muttering under her breath while Ragan shook the place down. He struck it rich. Lewis had enough guns in the house to start a civil war. Three Service Colt .45's and a tommy gun.

That was all Ragan needed. He dialed Headquarters and told them to come down and to bring along a warrant for Valentine Lewis. Any ex-convict with a gun in his possession was on his way back to jail.

Blue Eyes stood there looking mean. "You think you're smart, don't you?" she snapped finally.

That turned Ragan around. "Baby," he said, "whatever I am, I'm not dope enough to buck the law."

"No," she said, sneering, "you're just a dope. A first-class dope. You cops aren't smart enough to make any money for yourselves, so you just crab it for others."

"A cop doesn't have to be smart," Ragan explained gently, "although the mere fact that he's on the side of the law shows he's far from dumb. But a cop doesn't have to be smart because he's got organization, records of crimes and methods of operation, finger prints and photographs. He's got organizations in every city, he's got the help of the FBI, and, honey, you can't beat organization."

"You'd better have a squad when you go after Val," she said venemously. "I'd like to see you try it!"

The police cars were even then drawing up in front. "Lady," Ragan said, "that's just what I'm going to do, get him alone. He works in the Upshaw Building, doesn't he?"

Her surprise showed he was right. "Well," Ragan continued, "I am going to send you down to Headquarters, and then I'm going after your Val. In case you don't know, he slugged me last night. Now it's my turn!"

Her eyes widened. "Oh? So you're Joe Ragan," she said. Then her face stiffened, realizing she had made a miscue. "I hope he burns you down!"

Mark Stigler was with them when they came in. He looked grimly at the assortment of guns. "That would have outfitted half the crooks in America," he said angrily. Then he looked up at Ragan. "What is this? I thought you were going to break that Burns murder?"

Ragan's eyes turned to the girl. "This is part of it," he said. "See what this girl has to say. I don't think she wants to be an accessory."

She was really frightened now, but Stigler was still looking at Ragan. "You think this Val Lewis did it?"

"If he didn't, he knows who did."

All the way up to the Upshaw Building Stigler sat there chewing his cigar while Ragan gave it to him, fast and straight. All but the guy who did it. He built up the blackmail background, told him how Ollie had been worried by the Towne suicide, how he had worried at the problem like a dog over a bone. How Ragan's idea was that Ollie had been murdered because he stumbled into something really big, a blackmail ring.

He explained about the Bradford office, the letters dropped there, and the people who dropped them. Only one thing he left out. He said nothing about Angie. She was Ragan's girl, and he was still going to bat for her. She was being blackmailed and if he could cover for her, he would.

"You think they dropped money in those envelopes?"

"That's right."

"Find any of it to prove your theory?"

"No," Ragan admitted, "I didn't. I think all of those records in those filing cabinets, with the exception of a few well-known company names, are blackmail cases. I think from what I can remember of those files that the take must have run into thousands of dollars a month. They weren't bleeding just big shots—they were bleeding husbands and wives, clerks, stenographers, beauty operators, everybody, and the take was just rolling in. I think this Bradford, whoever he was, was a smart operator, but I think he had somebody else with him. Somebody who knew Ollie."

"Somebody who could get close to him?"

"Yes, and somebody who knew Ollie was getting close to the solution. Also, somebody who could get into his house after that gun or get it from his locker."

Stigler rolled his cigar in his lips. "You're doing a lot of talking," he said grimly. "It sounds good, but you've got to have the evidence!"

At the Upshaw Building, Stigler loitered around the corner of the hall and let Ragan go up after Val Lewis. Lewis was sitting there in his door where he had been before. As Ragan turned toward the door of the Bradford office Lewis got up and came around his desk. "What do you want?"

"What business is it of yours?" Ragan said. "I want into this office. Also—I want you for assault and murder!"

Lewis was too hot-headed for his own good. He started a punch, and it came fast. But Ragan rolled his head and slammed a right into Lewis' belly that jerked his mouth open, and then he hooked a left to the bridge of Lewis' nose. The nose folded under his fist like a wad of paper.

He was a big bruiser, bigger than Ragan, and built like an All-American half, but the fight was out of him. Stigler walked up a moment later. "You got a key to this place?" he demanded.

"No, I ain't!" Lewis said sullenly. "Bradford's got it."

"To hell with that!" Ragan's foot came up and he smashed his heel against the door jamb. A second time, then a third. It broke loose and he put his shoulder against it and pushed it open. While a harness cop took Val down the hall, he opened the filing cabinet.

It was empty.

A second and a third were empty too. Mark Stigler looked from Ragan to the smashed door. "Boy, oh, boy!" he said. "This is the prize! Now what?"

Ragan stood there, feeling sick. The files had been removed some time after he'd left the place. By now they were hidden or destroyed. And there was going to be a lot of explaining to do about this door. Stigler glared at him. "When you pull a boner, Joe, you sure pull a Lulu!"

"Mark," Ragan said, "do something for me. Get the lab busy on that floor. This is where Keene was murdered. Right there."

"How do you know?" Stigler demanded.

Ragan swallowed. "Because I was in here last night after the murder."

Stigler's eyes were like grey gimlets. "You were in here last night *after* the murder? Were you that prowler?"

"No," Ragan said, and gave it to him, everything, his meeting with Keene, his return, his finding the body, and the mysterious watcher outside.

"You got any idea who that was?" Stigler demanded. His eyes were fixed coldly on Ragan.

Ragan hesitated. "Maybe I have. But I don't want to say now."

CHAPTER FIVE

Knife-Fighter

Oddly, Stigler didn't follow that up. He just looked at Ragan and then he walked around the office, looking into this and then that. He was still puttering around when Ragan looked up to see the blonde in the door. "Hi, honey," she said cheerfully. "This is the first time I ever saw this door open."

"Who you working for now?" Ragan asked.

She smiled. "Nobody," she said. "I'm out of a job. Need a secretary?"

I grinned. "Lady, I could always find a place for you!"

Stigler turned around and looked at her from under his heavy brows. Then he rolled his cigar. "What do you know about this Bradford?" he demanded.

"Bradford?" Her eyes sharpened. "Why, I know plenty. Will it do"—she nodded toward Ragan—"him any good if I talk?"

"Plenty," Stigler said with emphasis.

"All right, then." She was suddenly all business. "I know that the man who has been calling himself Bradford for the past three months is not the Bradford who opened this office. He is a taller, broader, younger man.

"Furthermore, I know he was in my office last night after closing hours and must have been there after Mr. Keene was murdered."

Stigler took his cigar out of his mouth and stared. "How do you figure that?"

"Look." She crossed to the water cooler, and from the waste basket below it picked out a paper cup. "The man who calls himself Bradford has strong fingers. When he squeezes a paper cup after drinking, he shuts his right hand down on it, hard. He crushes it flat, then pushes the bottom up through the top a little way."

She picked up the waste basket and showed the half-dozen

cups to Stigler. He looked at them, then walked out and headed for Keene's office. She followed and picked up the basket under the cooler there. "See? One cup, left intact. That was Mr. Keene, and on top of it, above this paper that Mr. Keene threw away last night, a crushed cup."

Stigler chewed his cigar. "Lady," he said with genuine respect, "you'd make a copper."

Outside, in the street, Stigler said little. He was mulling something over in his mind. Ragan knew the man and knew he was bothered by something. Finally Stigler spoke. "Do you think those records were destroyed?"

"I doubt it," Ragan said. "If what that girl thinks is true, he hasn't been running this business long. He'd need the files to use himself."

Stigler nodded. "Joe, I don't know where you're getting, but you'll get some more time on it, and I won't push the case against Mary Burns until I hear more from you. In the meantime," he took the cigar from his mouth, "I think I'll check the unidentified dead and missing reports for the past three months."

Stigler got into his car and rolled away from the curb. Ragan stood there staring after him, and then realized that somebody was at his elbow. He turned. It was the blonde with the figure. "Can I help? I told you I was out of a job."

"Not unless you can remember something more about Bradford and that setup," Ragan said. "Did Keene know any more about them?"

"He was interested in a girl who came there," she said hesitantly, "and he had me follow her once."

"A girl? What sort of a girl?"

"A slender girl with red hair. She wore a green suit."

For a moment Ragan stood there looking at his cigarette. There was no sense in this, none at all. His mind turned to the blonde next to him. "What's your name, honey?" he asked after a minute.

"I wondered if you even cared," she said, smiling a little. Oddly, there was no humor in her eyes, just something faintly wistful and somehow very charming and very young. "It's Marcia Mahan," she said, "and I meant what I said about helping."

Somehow, now, Ragan didn't know what he wanted to do.

After all, there wasn't much evidence on Mary. Could they convict her? They had the testimony of Hazel Upton and Louella Chasen that she wanted a divorce, and of Angie Faherty that she had left the café for the rest room, but had not been in the rest room at the time of the killing.

The gun was Ollie's own, too. Yes, with work they could build a pretty stiff case against Mary. Quiet, lovely Mary Burns. No, Ragan could't step out now, no matter what happened. He owed it to Ollie. Ollie would have done as much for him. Yet now, suddenly, he began to see how it all was pointed, and the end he could see in sight made him feel sick and empty and helpless. One can control events only up to a point, and then the lives and feelings of other people enter in, and after that there is no longer any control.

Other things were clicking into place now. His memory was a good one, trained by police work, and he remembered suddenly something that he had forgotten. In those files there had been a company with the title Bysten Packing Company.

One of the big cases that Al Brooks had broken was that of Clyde Bysten. A blackmail case.

Ragan threw his cigarette into the gutter. "All right," he said. "If you want to help, you can. I want you to check on the insurance office," he noted down the address, "where Alice Towne worked. I want to have a list of the employees at that office during the time she worked there. Can you do that?"

Marcia nodded. "It will be easy."

"And meet me at the Peacock Bar at four."

Things would happen fast now, Ragan decided. Grabbing a cab, he headed for a bank. Within a matter of minutes he was closeted with the one vice president he knew there, and a few minutes later was getting the dope on an account. When he left that bank he felt as if he'd been kicked in the stomach.

Yet his job was only beginning, and from then until four he was busy checking back files of newspapers, using the telephone to save his legs, calling business firms, checking charge accounts and property lists. At the end of that time he had a formidable list of information, blackening information, that left him feeling worse than he could ever remember feeling in his life.

Outside that cocktail lounge, he stood waiting on the curb to finish his cigarette. The late afternoon sun was warm, and he was tired. He could see no end to what was coming. The night was going to be a busy one, for once more he was going to enter an apartment without a search warrant, only this time he was hoping he would find nothing. He was, in fact, going to enter two apartments.

Marcia was waiting for him, a bourbon and soda in front of her. She placed the list on the bar and Ragan scanned it. His heart almost stopped when he saw that name—the one he was almost positive he would see, and feared to see.

Marcia smiled at him. "You act as if you'd lost your best friend," she said. "Can I help?"

"Not right now," Ragan said. "But tonight you can."

She laughed. "I hope you don't mean what I think you do."

He chuckled. "Honey, this is business tonight, strictly business."

When Ragan came into the Homicide Division, Stigler was behind his desk. "Think I've got it," he said, shoving a card at Ragan. "Sam Bayless. He did two stretches for confidence games and was hooked into one blackmailing deal which couldn't be pinned on him. Smooth operator, fits the description we have of Bradford."

"Dead?"

"Yes. He was found shot to death in the desert near Palmdale. Shot four times through the chest with a .38. We have one of the slugs."

"Good deal!" Ragan looked at him. "Can you check it with that gun?"

"We will, somehow." Stigler chewed his cigar. "Have you got anything more?"

"Too much." Ragan hesitated. "He's not in this alone. He's got help. A woman."

Stigler rolled his cigar in his lips. "I had a hunch," he said. "You know who she is?"

Ragan nodded. "Before the night's over, I think we can cinch this case," he said quietly. "I'm going to look around now."

*　　*　　*

It was his duty, his duty as a police officer and to the memory of Ollie Burns, a good friend and a square cop, but he felt like a traitor. It was late when he went to the place near the park and stopped the car. For the purpose he had rented a car, and with Marcia Mahan there with him, they would look like any couple necking. They sat there, and Ragan was quiet. Too quiet.

"What do you want me to do when you go in?" she asked.

"Sit still. If they come back, push the horn button."

The door of the apartment house opened and a man and woman came out laughing and got into the car. Ragan saw the man's face. It was Al Brooks, hard, reckless, confident. He didn't want to look at the girl, but he had to. He knew who it would be. Angie Faherty.

For an instant her face was full under the street light and Ragan saw her eyes come toward his car. She said something softly to Brooks. Ragan turned toward Marcia. "Come on, honey, and make it look good."

She did. She came into his arms as if she belonged there and had been there for years, and the first time her lips met his the hair curled all the way to the top of his head.

Brooks came across the street toward the car and flashed a light on them, but Ragan's face was out of sight against her shoulder, and Marcia pulled her head up long enough to say, "Beat it, bud! Can't you see we're busy?"

Brooks chuckled and walked away. Ragan heard him make some laughing remark to Angie, and then they were driving off.

Marcia unwound herself. "Well!" she said after a minute. "If this is the kind of work detectives do . . ."

"Come here," Ragan said cheerfully. "They might come back. I think we'd better give them at least fifteen minutes of leeway. They might forget something and come back."

"I think," Marcia said dryly, "that you'd better go on inside and see what you don't want to see. I'll wait."

Opening the door was no trick. Once inside Ragan took a quick look around. It was all very familiar. Too familiar. Even to the picture of himself on the piano. That picture must have given Brooks many a good laugh.

The search was fast, thorough and successful. The files were

there, lying in plain sight on a shelf in the closet. He took them
down and was bundling them up when the horn honked.

They must have come fast, because when he swung around the
key was already in the lock. Ragan grabbed up the files. One
handful slipped and he ducked to grab it and the door slammed
open. Al Brooks, his face livid, stood framed in the door.

Slowly, Ragan put the files down. "Well, Al," he said, "here
it is. You've been waiting for this."

"Sure," Brooks said. There was concentrated hatred in the
man's eyes. "And I'm going to like it!"

He had his gun in his hand, and Ragan knew the man was
going to kill. But he wasn't going to kill Ragan without Ragan
putting up a struggle.

Brooks fired, and something burned Ragan along the ribs.
Ragan knocked him back over a chair and went over after him.
They came up slugging. Brooks came in throwing them with both
hands and caught Ragan with a wicked right that jarred clear to
Ragan's heels, and then an overhand left that smashed his ear and
made his head ring like a church bell.

Ragan had not been a fast light heavy for nothing, and punches
had been in his line of business. He took those two going in and
smashed a left and right to the body. Brooks backed up, and
Ragan hooked a wicked left to his mouth that smeared it into
bloody shreds, then dropped a right down the groove. Brooks
ducked to keep his chin away from that payoff punch and took it
over the eye. It cut to the bone and started the blood down his
face in a shower.

Shoving him away, Ragan swung again. Brooks jerked up a
knee for Ragan's groin, but Ragan twisted away. Brooks jumped
him then. His weight turned Ragan around and he ran a forearm
across Ragan's throat. Grabbing the man's hand and elbow,
Ragan dropped to one knee and flipped him over his shoulder.
Brooks got up slowly from that one, and he looked a sight.

"What's the matter, chum?" Ragan said. "Can't you take it?
Come on, tough boy! You liked it, and you wanted it, and now
you're getting it!"

Brooks came in again, but Ragan smashed him under the chin
with the butt of his palm, then across the face with an elbow.
Brooks staggered, gagging, and tried to fight. Ragan got a hand-

ful of hair and jerked the face under it down into the top of his head, which he was jerking up, hard. A nice touch, but hard on the features.

The door smashed open and Ragan looked up. It was Mark Stigler with a squad, Casey in the lead. "Got him?" Stigler asked. Then he saw Brooks. "Man, oh, man!" he said with admiration. "What did you use on him? A cleaver?"

"There's the files," Ragan said, indicating the heap where he had dropped them. "You'll find the Towne, Chasen and Upton payoffs there, and probably a lot more."

He looked toward the door. "Did you—I mean—well, what happened to Angie?"

"She's in the next room," Stigler said. "That blonde is with her."

It took Ragan a minute to get his heart slowed down to where he could walk inside. Angie Faherty did not look as lovely as he'd remembered her. In fact, she looked venomous at the moment. Her hair was all out of shape and she had a cut on one cheek.

"What hit you?" Ragan demanded.

Marcia looked up, smiling pleasantly. "A girl named Mahan. She gave me trouble, and I socked her."

Angie said nothing at all, and it wasn't in Ragan to get tough. She had double-crossed him and helped to frame Mary Burns, and still it wasn't in him to hate her. "What made you pull a stunt like this?" he asked.

She looked up. "You can't prove anything. Not a thing. You can't tie me in with this!"

"Sure we can, Angie," he said gently. "It's all sewed up, tight and neat. You killed Ollie Burns, and then you smeared him with lipstick. With you, whom he trusted, he would have talked. It was Al called him, but you met him there after you got Mary called away. Mary thought you were in some kind of trouble, and when she came back and you were gone, she, out of the goodness of her heart, tried to cover for you. She never dreamed you had killed Ollie.

"You took the gun out of their home. That was what puzzled me, for I thought about Al Brooks, and knew when all was considered that he couldn't get it away from the house. Or have access to it. You did.

"You had a good setup after Brooks came in. We've even got that angle figured out. You were in it with Bayless, or Bradford, if you want to call him that. You worked with Alice Towne, and you got the information on her that Bayless used in blackmailing her.

"On one of his vice raids, Al Brooks picked up a lot of information, and somehow he got hep to what you and Bayless were doing, so he declared himself in. Then he killed Bayless and you two took over the show. He killed Keene when he caught him in the office after hours. Knifed him, then shot him to make it appeared to be suicide."

"Got it all figured out, haven't you?" Brooks sneered from the doorway. "We'll see about this when I get out!"

Stigler shook his head. "They don't get out of the gas chamber, Al. We got one of the bullets you put into Bayless. It checks exactly with your Police Special."

"He got the dope on the Latko and Bysten cases from his own blackmailing racket," Ragan added. "He had a good thing there."

Angie Faherty got to her feet. Her face was stiff and cold. "You won't pin that on me," she insisted.

"Angie," Ragan said, "I checked your bank account. I checked two other accounts you have, your charge accounts, the property you bought. We have all the information we need. We know where you lived. We know that your brother did time with Bayless."

"My brother?" Her face went a shade more pale. "What do you know about him?"

"That's easy, Angie," Ragan said gently. "We picked him up today. He was using the name Valentine Lewis. His girl friend talked, plenty."

Later, while they were booking Al Brooks and Angie, Brooks picked up a paper cup from the cooler and drank. Then he squeezed it into a flattened mass, and with his thumb pushed the bottom up through the crumpled cup. It was an unconscious gesture, and noticing it, Stigler rolled his cigar in his lips, and looked over at Ragan. Marcia was standing beside Ragan, her hand through his arm. "What about that officer's wife, Joe? Shouldn't we go see her?"

"You're right. Is it okay, Mark?"

"Sure thing," Stigler agreed. "You two go ahead."

Outside, the air was cool with the after feel of rain, and they walked down to the car and got in without saying much. "Mary's a good friend of yours, isn't she?" Marcia asked.

"One of the best."

"Will she like me?"

"She will, I know."

They rode on in silence for a few minutes. "How about dinner tomorrow, and a show?"

"All right, and we'll have the dinner at my place!" she said quickly.

Ragan hoped they'd never get to the show.

COLLECT FROM A CORPSE

Pike Ambler called the Department from the Fan Club at 10 in the morning, and Lieutenant Wells Reyerson turned it over to Joe Ragan. "Close this one up fast," he ordered, "but give me an air tight case."

Ragan nodded. With Captain Bob Dixon headed for early retirement Ryerson was acting in charge of the burglary detail. If he made a record his chances of taking Dixon's job were good.

He knew the Fan Club. A small club, working in the red, it had recently zoomed into popularity on the dancing of Luretta Pace. He was considering that when he arrived at the club with Sam Blythe and young Lew Ryerson. Sam was a veteran, Lew a tall young man with a narrow face and shrewd eyes. He had been only four months in the department.

Sam Blythe glanced at the hole chopped through the ceiling, then at the safe. "An easy one, Joe. Entry through the ceiling, a punch job on the safe, nothing touched but money, and the floor swept clean after the job was finished." He walked over to the waste basket and picked from it a crumpled wad of crackly paper. "And here's the potato chip sack—all the earmarks of a Pete Slonski job."

Ragan rubbed his jaw and said nothing, his eyes puzzled and probing.

"Slonski, all right," Ryerson agreed. "It checks with the modus operandi file, and it's as open and shut as the Smiley case. I'll call Headquarters and have them send out a pickup on Slonski."

"Take it easy," Ragan interrupted, "let's look this over. Something smells."

"What's the matter?" Lew Ryerson was like his brother, too impatient to get things done. "You can see Slonski written all over it, like Sam said."

"Yeah," Ragan was dubious, "it does look like it."

"It is it!" Ryerson replied flatly. "I'm going to call in."

"It won't do any good," Ragan said mildly. "I said something smelled and it does. This job would even fool Slonski—but he didn't do it."

Sam Blythe was puzzled, Ryerson irritated. "How can you be so sure?" Ryerson demanded. "It's obvious to me!"

"This isn't a Slonski job unless ghosts crack safes. Pete was killed last week in Kansas City."

"What?" There was shocked incredulity on Ryerson's face. "How do you know that?"

"It was in the papers. And as we have a charge against him, I wired the FBI. They had a check on the prints. It was Slonski, all right, dead as a herring."

Blythe scowled. "Then something *is* funny. I'd take an oath this was Pete Slonski."

"So would I," Ragan admitted, "but now I'm wondering about the Smiley case. He swears he's innocent, and if I ever saw a surprised man it was Smiley when I put the cuffs on him."

"Oh, he's guilty, all right!" Ryerson was positive. "Of course, he would say he was innocent, but that case checked too well, and you know you can go almost as much by a crook's method of operation as by his finger prints."

"Like this one, you mean?" Ragan gestured at the safe. "This was a Slonski job, but Slonski's dead and buried."

"Smiley has a long record," Blythe said uneasily. "I never placed any great faith in his going straight."

"Neither did I," Ragan agreed, "but five years and no trouble. He's bought a home, built up a business, and not even a traffic count against him."

"On the other hand," Ryerson insisted, "he needs money. Maybe he's just been playing it smart."

"Crooks aren't smart," Ragan objected, "no man who will take a chance on a stretch in the pen is smart. They all make mistakes. They can't beat their own little habits."

"Maybe we've found a smart one," Ryerson suggested, "maybe he used to work with Slonski and made this one look like him to cover up."

"Slonski worked alone," Blythe objected. "However, the

similarity may be an accident. Let's get some pictures and get along with it.''

Joe Ragan prowled restlessly while Ryerson got his pictures. Turning from the office he walked out through the empty bar, crossing the shadowed dance floor through the aisles of tables and stacked chairs. Mounting the steps from the street, he entered the studio from which entry had been gained to the office below.

The door had been unlocked with a skeleton key, or picked open. There was a reception room with walls covered by the pictures of sirens with shadows in the right places and bare shoulders. In the studio itself there was a camera, a few reflectors, a backdrop and assorted props. The hole had been cut through the dark room floor.

Squatting, he studied the workmanship with care. A paper match lay on the floor and he picked it up and after a glance, put it in his pocket. The hole would have taken an hour to cut, and as the club closed at 2, and the personnel left right after, the burglar must have entered between 3 and 5 in the morning.

Hearing footsteps, Ragan turned to see a plump and harassed photographer. Andre Gimp fluttered his hands. "Oh, this is awful! Simply awful! Who could have done it?''

"Don't let it bother you. Look around and see if anything is missing and be careful you don't forget and break a leg in that hole.''

Ragan walked to the door and paused, lighting a cigarette. He was a big man, a shade over six feet tall, his wide, thick shoulders and big hands made men look twice. His hair was always rumpled, and despite his size there was something surprisingly boyish looking about him.

Ryerson had borrowed him a few days before from the Homicide Squad, for Ragan had been the ace man on the burglary detail before he transferred to Homicide.

Ragan ran his fingers through his hair and returned to the club. He was remembering the stricken look on the face of Ruth Smiley when he arrested her husband. There had been a feeling then that something was wrong, yet detail for detail the Smiley job had checked as this one checked with Slonski.

Leaving Lew Ryerson and Sam Blythe to question Ambler, he returned to Headquarters. He was scowling thoughtfully when he walked into Wells Ryerson's office. The lieutenant looked up, his eyes sharp with annoyance. "Ragan, when will you learn to knock? What is it you want? I'm very busy!"

"Sorry," Ragan dropped into a chair. "Are you satisfied with the Smiley case?" Briefly then, he explained their findings at the Fan Club.

Wells Ryerson waited him out, his irritation obvious. "That has nothing to do with Smiley. The man had no alibi. He was seen near the crime within thirty minutes of the time. We know his record and that he needs money. The tools that did the job came from his shop. The D.A. is well satisfied and so am I."

Ragan leaned his thick forearms on the chair arms. "Nevertheless," he insisted, "I don't like it. This job today checks with Slonski, but he's dead, so where does that leave me with Smiley? Or with Blackie Miller or Ed Chalmers?"

Ryerson's anger and dislike were evident as he replied. "Ragan, I see what you're trying to do. You know Dixon is to retire and if you can mess up my promotion you might step up. Well, you go back to Homicide. We don't want you or anybody like you. As of this moment you're off the burglary detail."

Ragan shrugged. "Sorry you take it that way. I'm not bucking for your job. I asked for my transfer to Homicide, but I don't like to see an innocent man go to prison."

"Innocent!" Ryerson's contempt was thick. "You talk like a school boy! Jack Smiley was in the reform school when he was sixteen, and in the pen when he was twenty-four. He was short of cash and he reverted to type. Go peddle your papers in Homicide."

Joe Ragan closed the door behind him, his ears burning. He knew how Ryerson felt, but could not forget the face of Ruth Smiley, nor the facts that led to the arrest of her husband. Smiley, Miller and Chalmers had been arrested largely on information from the *modus operandi* file.

It was noon and lunch time. He hesitated to report to his own chief, Mark Stigler. Yet he was stopping his car before the white house on the side street off Melrose before he realized it.

Ruth Smiley had no welcoming smile when she opened the door. He removed his hat, flushing slightly. "Mrs. Smiley, I'd

like to ask a few questions if I may. It might help Jack if you'll
answer them.''

There was doubt in her eyes, but a flicker of hope, too.
"Look," he said, "something has come up that has me wondering.
If the Department knew I was here they wouldn't like it, as I'm
off this case, but I've a hunch." He hesitated. "Now, we know
Jack was near the scene of the crime that night. What was he
doing there?''

"We told you, Mr. Ragan. Jack had a call from the Chase
Printing Company. He repaired a press of theirs once and they
wanted him there not later than four o'clock as they had a rush
job to begin the following morning.''

"That was checked, and they said they made no such call.''

"Mr. Ragan," Ruth Smiley pleaded, "please believe me! I
heard him talking! I heard his replies!''

Ragan scowled unhappily. This was no help, but he was
determined now. "Don't raise your hopes," he said, "but I'm
working on an angle that may help.''

The Chase Printing Company was no help. All their presses
were working and they had not called Smiley. Yes, he had
repaired a press once, and an excellent job, too. Yes, his card
had been found under their door when they opened up.

Of course, the card could have been part of an alibi, but that
was one thing that had bothered him all along. "Those guys were
crooks," he muttered, "and yet none of them had an alibi. If
they had been working they would have had iron clad stories to
prove them elsewhere!''

Yet the alternative was a frame-up by someone familiar with
their working methods. A call had taken Smiley from his bed to
the vicinity of the crime, a crime that resembled his work! With
their records he would certainly be convicted.

He drove again to the Fan Club. Pike Ambler greeted him.
"Still looking? Have you any leads?''

"A couple." Ragan studied the man. "How much did you
lose?''

"Two grand three hundred. I can't take it, Joe." His brow
creased with worry. "Luretta hasn't been paid and she'll raise a
squawk you'll hear from here to Flatbush.''

"You mean Luretta Pace? Charlie Vent's girl?''

Ambler nodded. "She was Vent's girl before he got himself vented." He smiled feebly at the pun. "She's gone from one extreme to the other. Now it's a cop."

"Cop?" Ragan looked around at Ambler. "Who?"

"Lew Ryerson's dating her." Ambler shrugged. "I don't blame the guy. She's a number, all right."

Ragan returned to the office and reported, then completed some routine work. It was late when he finally got to bed.

He awakened with a start, the phone jangling in his ears. He grabbed it sleepily. "Homicide calling, Joe. Stigler said to give it to you."

"To me?" Ragan was only half awake. "Man, I'm off duty!"

"Yeah," the voice was dry, "but this call's from the Fan Club. Stigler said you'd want it."

He was wide awake now. "Who's dead?"

"Pike Ambler. He was shot just a few minutes ago. Get out there fast as you can."

Two patrol cars were outside and a cop was barring the door. He took his arm down to let Joe in and he walked back to the office. Ambler was lying on his face alongside the desk, wearing the cheap tux that was his official costume. His red face was drained of color now, the blue eyes vacant.

Ragan glanced around to the doctor. "How many times was he shot?"

"Three times, and damned good shooting. Two of them right through the heart at close range. Probably a .45."

"All right." Ragan glanced up as a man walked in. It was Sam Blythe. "What are you doing here?"

"Prowling. I was talking to the cop on the beat when we heard the shots. We busted in here, and he was lying like that, with the back window open. We went out and looked around but nobody was in the alley and we heard no car start."

"Who else was in the club?"

"Nobody. The place closed at two, and the last one to leave was that Pace gal. What a set of gams *she's* got!"

"All right. Have the boys round 'em all up and get them back here." He dropped into a chair when the body had been taken away and studied the situation, with Blythe watching him through lowered lids.

He got up, finally, and made a minute examination of the room, locating two of the three bullets and digging them from the wall. They were .45's all right. He studied them thoughtfully.

"You know," Blythe suggested suddenly, "somebody could be playing us for suckers. Kicking this *modus operandi* stuff around like they are."

"Could be." What was Blythe doing here at this hour? He got off at midnight. "Whoever it is has established a new method of operation. All these jobs, Smiley, Chalmers, Miller and this one, all between 3 to 5 a.m. The technique of other men, but his own working hours."

"You think those jobs were frames? Ryerson won't like it!"

Ragan shrugged. "I'd like to see his face when he finds I'm back on this case."

"You think it's the same one?" Blythe asked quickly.

"Don't you?" Blythe was shrewd.

"I don't know. Those were burglaries, this is murder."

"Sure," Ragan said, "but suppose Ambler suspected somebody otherwise not suspected? Wouldn't the crook have a motive for murder?"

A car slowed out front and then a door slammed open. They heard the click of angry heels and Luretta Pace swept into the room. Her long almond shaped eyes swept from Blythe to Ragan. "You've got a nerve!" she stormed. "Getting me out of bed in the middle of the night! Why couldn't you wait until tomorrow?"

"It is tomorrow," Ragan replied. He held out a crumpled pack of smokes. "Have one?"

She stared to refuse, but something in his amused gray eyes made her resentment flicker out. She turned abruptly, seated herself on the arm of a chair. "All right, ask your questions!" she flared.

She had green eyes and auburn hair. Ragan found himself liking it. "First," he suggested, "tell us about the fight you had with Ambler."

Luretta Pace stiffened and the warmth left her face. "Listen!" she protested sharply. "Don't try to frame me! I won't stand still for it! I was out of here before he was shot, and you know it!"

"Sure, I know it. And I don't think you slipped around back

and shot him through the rear window, either." He smiled at her. "Although you could have done it."

Her face paled, but Luretta had been fighting her own battles too long. "Do you think I'd kill a guy who owes me six hundred bucks? You don't collect from a corpse! Besides, Pike was a good lad. He was the first guy I'd worked for in a long time who treated me right."

"What about the fight?" Joe persisted.

"You'll hear about it, anyway," Luretta said. "Joe owed me money and couldn't pay up. The dough he figured on paying me was in that safe, so when he was robbed, I figured I was working for nothing. I can't afford that, so we had some words and I told him what he could do with his night club."

"Did he say when he could pay? Or tell you when he might have money?"

"Yes, as a matter of fact he said he would have it all back, every dime. He told me he would pay me tomorrow. I didn't believe him."

"Where do you think he planned to get it?"

"How should I know?" Luretta shrugged a rounded shoulder.

"Then," Ragan asked gently, "he said nothing about knowing who robbed him?"

Sam Blythe sat up abruptly, his eyes on Ragan's and Luretta lost her smile. She was suddenly serious. "No, not exactly, but I guess what I told you could be taken that way. Do you think that was why he was killed? Because he knew, and tried to get his money back?"

It was a theory and a good one. Suppose Ambler possessed information not available to the police, and believed he could get his money returned by promising not to turn in the thief? If he contacted the criminal, that would be a motive for murder. Joe realized there were other reasons for murder. He believed the relationship of Ambler and Luretta was strictly business, as they represented it—but suppose someone had not?

Yet the only admirer of Luretta's he knew was Lew Ryerson, and that was ridiculous. Or was it?

Such a girl as Luretta Pace would have many admirers. That

Sam Blythe thought she was really something was obvious. For that matter, he did, himself.

It was almost noon when he left the club and walked out into the sunlight, trying to assemble his thoughts and assay the value of what he had learned. He was standing on the curb when Andre Gimp came up to him. "Mr. Ragan," Gimp was fluttering again, "only one thing is missing, and it seems very strange, for it was only a picture."

"A picture?" Joe Ragan knew what was coming. "Of whom?"

"Luretta Pace—in costume!"

There it was again. The burglary, Luretta, the murder. He drove back to Headquarters and found Stigler pacing the floor with excitement. "Hey," Stigler exploded. "Look at this! You've really got something! *The gun that killed Ambler was the same that killed Charlie Vent!*"

"I thought so when I ordered them checked. A hunch I had."

"You think this ties up with the burglaries?" Stigler asked. Then he smiled. "Ryerson called up, boiling mad. Said you'd been questioning people. I told him Homicide had a hand in it now. He shut up like a clam, but he was sure sore." Stigler studied him. "What next?"

"A little looking around, then another talk with Luretta Pace."

In the alley back of the Fan Club he found where a man had been standing behind a telephone post watching Ambler through the window. A man who smoked several cigarettes and dropped paper matches. Ragan picked up a couple of them and each paper match stub had been divided at the bottom, parted by a thumb nail and bent back to form a cross. Such a thing a man might do unconsciously, while waiting.

Ragan stowed the matches in a white envelope with a notation as to where they were found. In another envelope was an identical match. And he knew where more could be found.

Later, he went to a small target range in the basement of Headquarters and fired a couple of shots, then collected all the bullets he could find in the bales of cotton that served as a back stop for the targets.

Luretta met him at the door when he arrived, and he smiled at her curious glance. "Wondering?" he asked.

"Wondering whether this call is business or social." She took his hat, then glanced over her shoulder. "Drink?"

"Bourbon and soda."

She was wearing sea green slacks and a pale yellow blouse. Her hair was down on her shoulders and it caught the sunlight. He leaned back in his chair and crossed his legs, watching her move about.

"Ever think about Charlie?" he asked suddenly.

The hand that held the bottle hesitated for the briefest instant. When she came to him with his drink and one of her own, she looked at him thoughtfully. "That's a curious thing to ask. Charlie's been dead for four, nearly five months."

"You didn't answer my question," Ragan said.

She looked over her glass at him. "Occasionally. He wasn't a bad sort, you know, and he really cared for me. But why bring him up?"

"Oh, just thinking!" The highball tasted good. He realized suddenly that he was sleepy. "I wondered if some of your most recent company had made you forget him."

Luretta looked him over carefully. "Joe," she said suddenly, "you're not subtle. Why don't you come right out and ask me what you want to know?"

"I wasn't trying to be subtle. The truth is, I've got a finger on something and it's pure dynamite. I can't do a thing until I know more or the whole thing is liable to fly up and hit me in the face.

"This I will say. Two things are tied up with the killing of Pike Ambler. One of them is these burglaries, and the other one is you."

"*Me?*" She laughed. "Oh, no, Joe! Don't tell me that! Why, it couldn't be! There was nothing between us, and you certainly don't think I double in robbing safes?"

"No, I don't. Nor do I think there was anything between you and Pike. It's what somebody else might think. Moreover, you may know more than you realize, and I believe if I could be inside your mind and memory, I could put the pieces together that would give me a murderer." He got to his feet and put his glass down. "If anybody should ask you, this call was purely social. If you're looking as lovely as you do now, it would be easy to believe!"

The buzzer sounded from the door, and when she opened it, Lew Ryerson stood there, his eyes going from her to Ragan. He seemed about to speak, but Ragan beat him to it. "Hi, Lew! Nice to see you."

Ryerson came on into the room, his eyes holding Ragan's. "Heard you were wrapped up in a murder case?"

"Yeah, but I took time off to drop around for a drink."

"Looks like I've got competition." There was no humor in the way he said it, and his eyes were cold, measuring.

"With a girl like Luretta you'll always have it."

Ryerson looked at her, his lips thinned down. "I guess that's so," he said, "but that doesn't make me like the idea any better."

She followed Ragan to the door. "Don't mind him, and do come back!"

There was ugly anger in Ryerson's eyes. "Luretta," he said, "I want you to tell him not to come back!"

"Why, I won't do anything of the kind!" She turned on Lew. "We're only dating occasionally, Lew. I told you after Charlie was killed that it wouldn't be any different. I just wasn't tying myself down. If Mr. Ragan wants to come back, he's welcome!"

"Thanks, honey," Ragan turned to Lew. "See you later, Lew. It's all fun, you know?"

Ryerson glared. "Is it?" he demanded. "I'm not so sure."

Sam Blythe was waiting for him when he walked into the office at Homicide. His face was dark and angry. "What goes on here?" he demanded. "Who gave you the right to have my gun tested by Ballistics?"

"Nobody," Joe admitted cheerfully. "I knew you didn't carry it off duty, and figured I'd have it checked. I had mine checked, too, and Stigler's."

"What?" Stigler glared. "You had Ballistics check my gun?"

"Sure!" Ragan dropped on a corner of the desk. "I had to have some dope, and now I've got it."

"Aside from fooling around, how are you coming with the Ambler case? Have you found the murderer?"

"Sure I have."

Stigler jumped and Blythe brought his leg down from the arm of his chair. "Did you say—you have? You *know* who did it?"

"That's right. I know who did it, and that means I know who killed Charlie Vent, too."

He scowled suddenly, and picked the phone from its cradle, dialing a number. Luretta answered. "Joe here," he said, "still busy?"

"Yes."

"Luretta, I wanted to tell you but forgot. The same man who killed Pike Ambler killed Charlie Vent."

"What?" He heard her astonished gasp, but before she could ask questions, he interrupted.

"Honey, don't ask any questions now, or make any comments, but you do some thinking, and then call me, any time of the day or night."

He replaced the phone and turned back to Stigler, who took the cigar from his mouth. "All right, give! Who did it?"

"Stigler," Ragan leaned back against the desk, "you'd call me a liar if I told you. Nor have I evidence enough for a conviction, but I've arranged a trap for him if he'll only walk into it. Also, he pulled those jobs for which Blackie Miller, Ed Chalmers and Jack Smiley are now awaiting trial!"

"That's impossible!" Stigler protested, but Ragan knew he believed. Sam Blythe sat back in his chair watching Ragan and saying nothing, his eyes cold and curious.

"Well, then. What happens now?" Stigler demanded.

"We sit tight. I've some more prowling to do."

"What if your killer lams? I want this case sewed up, Ragan!"

"Just what Wells Ryerson told me. You'll both get it." Ragan studied his shoes. "Anything about Charlie Vent's murder ever puzzle you, Chief? You'll recall that he was shot three times in the face, and that's not a normal way to kill a man."

"I've thought of that. If it hadn't been a gang killing, I'd say it was jealousy or hate."

"That's my idea. Somebody wanted to take over, all right, but the muscle was on Charlie's girl, not the rackets."

"That doesn't make sense," Blythe protested. "Lew Ryerson is going with her."

"And how many other guys?" Ragan asked. "She's a doll, that one."

"Yeah," Sam agreed dryly, "I could name three of them right now."

The phone rang. Ragan dropped a hand to it, lifting it. "Joe, this is Luretta. I think I know what you mean. Can you come over about ten tonight?"

"Sure, and not a minute late." He hung up and glanced around at them. "That's a date for ten, and I think we'll get all the evidence we need. If you guys can sit in a car and wait for awhile, I'll give you a murderer."

It was dark under the row of trees along the curb opposite the apartment house where Luretta Pace lived, and the dark, un-marked car was apparently empty. Only a walker along the walk between the·park fence and the trees might have seen the three men who sat in the car.

"You're sure this deal is set right, Joe? We can't slip now!"

"It's set. Just sit tight and wait."

Rain began to fall, whispering on the leaves and the car top. It was almost 8:40 when Ragan suddenly touched Stigler on the sleeve. "Look!" he whispered.

A man had come around the corner out of the side street near the apartment house. He wore a raincoat and his hat brim was pulled down. He stepped quickly into the door.

Mark Stigler sat straight up. "Man, that looked just like—!" His voice faded as he met Ragan's eyes.

"It was!" Ragan replied, grimly.

A curtain in an apartment house window went up and down rapidly, three times. "Let's go," Ragan said, "we've got to hurry."

An officer in uniform admitted them to the apartment next door to that of Luretta Pace. A recording was already being made, and through the hidden mike in the next apartment they could hear the voices, hear them plainly.

"—I don't care who he is!" A man was speaking, a voice that stiffened Sam Blythe to the same realization that had touched Mark Stigler on the outside. "Keep him away from here!"

"I don't intend to keep anyone away whom I like. As a matter of fact, I don't care for him."

"Then tell him so!"

"Why don't you tell him?" Luretta's voice was taunting. "Are you afraid? Or won't he listen to you?"

"Afraid? Of course not! Still, it wouldn't be a good idea. I'd rather he not know we're acquainted."

"You weren't always so hesitant."

"What do you mean by that?"

"Why, you never approved of Charlie, either. You knew I liked him, but you didn't want me to like him."

"That's right. I didn't."

"One thing I'll say for Charlie. He was a good spender. I don't really care whether a man spends money on me or not, but it helps. And Charlie did."

"You mean that I don't? I think I've been pretty nice, lately."

"Lately. Sometimes I wonder how you do it on your salary."

"I manage."

"As you managed a lot of other things? Like Charlie, for instance?"

There was no sound, then the man's voice, lower and colder. "Just what do you mean by that?"

"Well, didn't you? You didn't really believe that I thought he was killed in a gang war, did you? Nobody wanted Charlie dead—nobody but you."

The man laughed. "I always did like a smart girl! Well, now you know the sort of man I am, and you know just how we stand, and what I can do to you or anyone. The best of it is, they can't touch me!"

There was a sound of a glass put down on a table. "Luretta, let's drop this nonsense and get married. I'm going places and nothing can stop me."

"No, I won't marry you. This has gone far enough as it is." Luretta's voice changed. "You'd better go now. I never knew just what sort of person you were, although I always suspected. At first, I believed you were making things easy for me by not allowing too many questions, but now I realize you were protecting yourself."

"Naturally! But I was protecting you, too."

Joe Ragan got up and took his gun from the shoulder holster and slid it into his waist band. Blythe was already at the door. His jaw was set hard.

"I neither wanted nor needed protection," Luretta was saying, "I cared for Charlie. I want you to know that. No, I wasn't in love with him, but he was good to me, and I hadn't any idea that you killed him. If I had, I'd never have spoken to you. Now get out!"

The man laughed. "Don't be silly! We're staying together, especially now."

"What do you mean?"

"Why, I wouldn't dare let you go now. We'll either get along together or you'll get what Charlie got." There was a bump as of a chair knocked over and a shout. *"Stay away from that door!"*

Ragan was moving fast, his face white. He swung into the hall and gripped the knob, but it was locked. There was a crash inside, and in a sudden fury of fear for the girl, he dropped his shoulder against the door in a lunge. The lock broke and he stumbled into the room.

Lieutenant Wells Ryerson threw the girl from him and grabbed his gun, but Ragan came too fast. Slapping the gun aside, he smashed a right to the chin, then a left. Ryerson fell backward, firing as he fell, then scrambled to his feet, lifting his gun.

Joe Ragan drew and fired in the same instant and his shot slammed Ryerson back against the wall, while the other bullet buried itself harmlessly in the wall. The gun dribbled from Ryerson's fingers and he slipped to the floor.

His eyes opened and for a moment as they met Ragan's they were sharp, clear and intelligent. "I told you," he said hoarsely, "to close this one up fast. An air—tight case."

His voice faded, and then he fought for air, and whispered, "It looked so—easy! The file—those—those ex-cons on the loose. I—I could make—record, and—money, too."

He seemed to catch his breath, then exhaled slowly. He did not inhale again.

Mark Stigler stared at him. "Ryerson! Who would ever have believed it!" He glanced at Ragan, who stood with Luretta's face buried against his shoulder. "What tipped you off?"

Ragan waved a hand. "It had to be somebody with access to

the *modus operandi* file, and who could be out between three and five a.m. It couldn't be you, Mark, because your wife wouldn't stand for it. And Sam likes his sleep too well, but what really tipped me off was this," he picked up a split paper match from an ash tray. "It was a habit he had of splitting the end of those matches.

"Matches like that were found on the Smiley and Miller jobs, and I found some in the alley near Ambler's office."

"Did Lew know his brother liked Luretta?"

"I doubt it."

"What about Ambler?"

"I think he knew. And somehow he knew that it was Wells Ryerson who cracked his safe, and he must have called him. Ryerson didn't dare return it for then there would always be someone who knew his secret."

When the body had been taken away, Stigler looked over to Ragan. "Coming with us, Joe? Or are you staying?"

"Neither! We're going to see Ruth Smiley, and I want that to be the first thing you do. Turn him loose."

"She'll be so happy!" Luretta said, when they were in the car. "It must be wonderful to make someone that happy!"

He chuckled. "You'll find out, honey! You'll find out!"

STAY OUT OF MY NIGHTMARE!

CHAPTER ONE

Gun Girl

When I walked in Bill looked up. "There was a guy in here looking for you. A young fellow about twenty-five or so. He said to tell you it was Bradley."

"What did he want? Did he say?" As I spoke I took a quick gander around the bar to see if any of my crowd were in. None of them was, but there was a fellow four or five stools away with slick hair and a pasty face. He looked as if he was on the weed.

"He just wanted to see you, but he wanted you bad."

Bill brought me a bourbon and soda and I thought it over a little. Sam Bradley had been a corporal in my platoon overseas, but we had not seen each other since our return. We had talked over the phone, but somehow we had never come to the point of meeting. I knew that if he wanted to see me badly there was something definitely wrong.

He was a nice guy, Sam was. A good, reliable man and one of the nicest fellows I'd ever met. "I'll look him up," I said. "Maybe he's in trouble. He's a right guy."

"You never can tell," the man with the sickly face interrupted. "Right guys turn out wrong sometimes. I wouldn't trust my best friend."

The interruption irritated me. "You know your friends better than I do," I told him.

He looked around at me and there was nothing nice about his expression. Furthermore when I looked directly into his eyes I changed my mind about him. This fellow was no casual bar rat with a couple of drinks under his belt and wanting to work off a grouch. This guy was poison.

That look was one I'd seen before, and usually the man who wore it was a killer. It was the look of a man who understands only brutality and cruelty. "That sounded like a crack," he said, looking me over.

"Take it any way you like," I said. "I didn't ask you into the conversation."

"You're a big guy," he said, watching me like a snake watching a bird, "and I don't like big guys. They always think they've got the edge on you. And you're just like the rest of them. But maybe I could bring you down to my size."

He was making me sore. I was asking for no trouble, and had no idea of anything like trouble when I walked into the Plaza. Sam Bradley was on my mind, and I'd no idea of messing around with any specimen like this. "Your size?" I said. "They just don't get that small. Nothing is that low."

When he came off that stool I knew he meant business. Some men bluff. This torpedo didn't. He was going to kill me. Yet he was only a step away from me when I saw the shiv. He was holding it low down in his right hand, and nobody in the bar could see it but me. He might have been hitting the weed, but he was smart, this one was.

"Put the shiv away, chum." I had not moved from the stool. "You tackle me with that and they'll be putting you on ice before dark. I don't like steel."

He never said a word. He just stood there looking at me with those flat, ugly eyes. Bill heard me speak of the knife and came down the bar, always ready to stop anything that meant trouble, and to stop it if he could before it started.

"Don't do it, pal," I said. "They've got a new carpet on the deck. I don't want to smear it with you."

He came in then, so fast he nearly got me. Nearly, but not quite. His right foot was forward, and when that knife licked out like a snake's tongue I chopped his wrist and hand to deflect the point of the blade. My hand then closed on his wrist and jerked him toward me to get him off balance. Then I shoved back quick and at the same moment caught him behind the knee with my foot.

He went down hard, the knife flying from his hand and his head thudding on the brass trough at the base of the bar. I picked up the knife and tossed it to Bill. "Cute thing," I said. "Start a collection. I've got mine."

Getting off the stool I walked out of the bar into the afternoon sunlight. Cops might come around and there was no use straining Mooney's friendship any further. Grabbing a cab I headed for Bradley's place.

It was a single off Wilshire and in a nice neighborhood. When I pressed the bell nothing happened. Ellen must be shopping. Bradley would be at work, probably. I tried the bell once again for luck and was turning away when I spotted the white edge of a calling card sticking out from beneath the door. It was none of my business, but I stooped down and pulled it out. It read: Edward Pollard, Attorney at Law.

Under it in a crabbed, tight-fisted script were the words:

Was here at eight as you suggested. If you return before ten P.M. meet me at Merrano's. Don't do anything or talk to anyone until I see you.

Pollard was not unknown to me. He was a shyster who handled bail bonds and some criminal cases. We had never met, however. But I also knew Merrano's which was a night club on a side street, a small, out-of-the-way club, but well appointed and catering to a clientele on the fringe of the underworld.

Yet what impressed me about the card was not that. It was the fact that this card seemed evidence that neither Sam nor his wife had been home since the previous night. Where then, was Sam? And where was Ellen?

Reaching the walk, I stopped there, thrusting the card down into my coat pocket. At that moment a four-door sedan wheeled up to the curb and a man got out hurriedly. He brushed by me without a glance and went right to Bradley's door. He didn't ring the bell or knock, but stooped quickly and began to look for something on the step or under the door. Then he knelt and tried to look under the door. Getting to his feet, he tried the knob, but it was locked. Only then did he press the bell. Even as he did so, however, he was turning away as if sure it would not be answered.

He gave me a quick look as he saw me watching him, then started by. "Hello, Pollard," I said.

He stopped as if struck and turned sharply around to me. His quick, ratty eyes went over me, his face tightening. "Who are you? I never saw you before." He had a quick, nervous voice and was obviously a very worried man.

"The name is Morgan. I was just wondering why a man would try a door before ringing the bell, and why he should make a careful inspection of the step before trying the door."

"It's none of your business, young man!" he said testily. "It strikes me that you've little to do, standing around prying into people's affairs!"

He did not move, however. He was worried, and he was waiting to see what my angle was. So far he had not decided what I was or what I meant to him.

For that matter, neither had I. Actually I had no business stopping him. Sam Bradley and his wife might be visiting. There was no sense in building elaborate plots over nothing, yet the fact that Sam wanted to see me so badly, and that I had found the card of such a man as Pollard under his door was disturbing.

Two facts had been evident. Pollard had not expected Sam to be home, and he had wanted to pick up his card. He couldn't have been looking for anything else.

That made sense, of a sort. If Pollard believed Sam wasn't home, it might mean that he knew where he was. And why would he go to all the trouble to return for his card, unless there was something wrong?

"Look, pal," I said, "suppose you tell me where Sam is and why you were so sure he wasn't home. What's the dope?"

"It's none of your business!" he said angrily. He turned away and I let him take two steps before I spoke.

"Sam Bradley is a friend of mine. I hope nothing has happened to him, or will happen to him. From your actions I am beginning to wonder, and if anything has happened to him, I am not only going to see that the police ask questions, but I'm going to ask some myself—and, buddy, I'll get answers!"

That took him right where he lived. He hurried to the car and got in. He rolled down the window and leaned back as if to speak, then started off with a jerk. There was just time enough to catch his license number before he got away.

Standing there in the street I thought it over. I had nothing to go on but some suspicions, and those didn't have much foundation.

Telling myself I was a fool and that Sam would not appreciate it, I walked back up to the door. The lock was no trick for me, for I'd been a locksmith for several years, and in something over a minute I was inside.

The apartment was empty. Hoping Sam would forgive me, I made a hurried check. The beds were unslept in, the garbage unemptied, yet there were no dirty dishes.

Checking the top drawer of the bureau, I found something. It was a stack of neatly pressed handkerchiefs, but some of them had been laid aside and something taken from between them. There was a small spot of oil and the imprint of something that had been resting there for some time. That something had apparently been an Army .45 Colt.

My thoughts were interrupted by the rattle of a key in the door, and I hurriedly closed the drawer and stepped to the door of the bedroom, just in time to see the door close behind a girl.

Her eyes widened and she stopped, as if uncertain how to proceed. She was uncommonly pretty, and that contributed to my surprise, for I had seen Ellen Bradley's picture, and this was not she.

Turning as if to be sure the door was shut tightly, her bag slipped from her fingers. My eyes followed it, and then I looked up into the muzzle of a .32 automatic. "Who are you?" she demanded. "What are you doing here?"

It had been a neat trick. That bag had dropped, and she had dropped it purposely to distract me. There was nothing distracting about that gun. It was steady and it was ugly. Whoever this girl was, she was obviously an old hand, and one with a quick, agile brain. "Who are you?" she repeated.

"Let's say then that I'm an old Army friend of Sam Bradley's."

Her eyes hardened a little. "Oh, so that's it. You admit you're one of them?" Before I could reply, she added, "I believe I'll call the police."

"It might be a good idea," I agreed, "but why don't you put that gun down and we can talk this over. Sam left word that he wanted to see me, and if you're a friend of his maybe we should compare notes. I hurried right over when I heard from him. I thought he must be in trouble."

"I'll bet you did!" she said. "Now back up against the wall.

I'm going to use the telephone and if you have any doubts that I'll use this gun, just start something."

I had no doubts.

She took the receiver off the cradle and dialed a number. I watched the spots she was dialing and filed it away for future use. From where I stood I could hear a voice speak, but could distinguish no words.

Then the girl said, "Yes, Harry, I'm at Sam's. . . . No, no sign of him, but there's somebody else here." She listened and I could hear Harry's voice talking rapidly. She looked me up and down coolly. "Big fellow, over six feet and broad shouldered. Grey suit, blue shirt and gray tie. Good looking but stupid. And," she added, "he got in without a key."

She listened a minute. "Hold him? All right. Of course, I will! I'll not miss, either. I always," she said, "shoot for the stomach. They don't like it there."

She replaced the telephone and perched on the edge of a table. "You might as well sit down. They won't be here for ten minutes." She studied me as if she were looking at an insect. "A friend of Sam's, eh? I know how friendly you guys are. What are you trying to do—cut in?"

"Cut in on what?" I asked.

She smiled. "Subtle as a truck. As if you didn't know!"

"And who," I asked, "is Harry?"

"He's a friend of mine, and from what he said over the phone I think he knows you. And he doesn't like you."

"I'm worried," I said. "That really troubles me. Now, give: What's all this about? Where's Sam? Where's Ellen? What's happened to them?"

"Don't kid me—you know all about it!" Her voice was bitter, and it puzzled me. Not to say I wasn't puzzled about the whole thing. Sam Bradley was in plenty of trouble, without a doubt, but what sort of trouble?

Despite the fact that something in her attitude made me wonder if she were not friendly to Sam and Ellen, she had come in with a key and she had not called the police. Moreover, she was handling this situation with vastly more assurance than one would expect from the average woman. It was an assurance that spoke of familiarity with guns and handlers of guns. Another thing I knew: The number she dialed was not that of the police department.

"Look," I said, "if you're a friend of Sam's we had better compare notes. When he left here he took a gun. If Sam has a gun you can bet he's getting desperate, because it isn't like him."

At the mention of the gun her face tightened. "A gun? How do you know?"

I explained. "Now tell me," I finished, "what this is all about."

Before she could reply, hurried footsteps sounded on the walk and she got up and stepped back to the door. She opened it, but her eyes showed uncertainty, even fear.

CHAPTER TWO

Corpses Can't Confess

Three men stepped into the room and when I saw them every fiber in my being turned cold. There wasn't a cop in the country who wouldn't love to get his hands on George Homan. He was the first man through the door, and when my eyes fell on him I lost the last bit of hope I had that this girl might be friendly. No girl who knew Homan could be friend to any honest man. Homan was a brutal killer, cold blooded and utterly vicious.

The second man I didn't know. He was tall, with a wiry body and broad shoulders, his features were sharp and his brows a straight bar of black above his deep-set eyes. Then I saw the last man. It was my friend from the bar, the man who had tried to knife me. Now I knew why he wanted my scalp. It was because he had heard me say I was going to find out what Sam's trouble was.

"This is the one, Harry," the girl was saying to him. "He claims he's a friend of Bradley's."

Harry walked slowly over to me, his bright, rodent-like eyes on mine, the hatred in them sharpened now by triumph.

"Nice company you keep." I said, looking past him at the girl. "Did he ever show you the frog sticker he carries? Anyway, I know now where you stand. No girl who was a friend of Sam's would ever know a rat like this!"

"Shut your face!" Harry yelled, his mouth twisted with viciousness, and as he spoke, he swung.

It was the wrong thing to do. Gun or no gun, I was in no mood to get hit. For a second, Harry had stepped between me and the gun, but as he stepped in, throwing his right, I dropped my left palm to his shoulder, stopping the punch, and then I brought one from the hip into his mid-section that had the works on it.

His mouth fell open and his face turned green as he gagged and gasped for breath.

Before he could fall, I jumped in close, grabbing him by the shoulders, and shoved him hard at Homan. The third man I didn't know, but George was no bargain and I wanted him out of the play. I went for my gun fast. Hatchet Face had also yanked out his gun, but neither of us fired. We just stood there, staring at each other. It was a Mexican stand-off. If either of us fired at that range we both would die.

The girl had not moved except to drop the gun to her side. She seemed petrified, staring at me as if a light had suddenly been flashed in her eyes.

Homan had backed away from Harry who was groaning on the floor. Livid hate flashed in Homan's eyes. "Kill him, Pete!" His voice was hoarse with emotion. "Kill him!"

"Sure," I said, "he can kill me if he wants to ride the same slide to the hot place. Shoot, but all of you go with me. I'm a big guy, and it's going to take a lot of lead if you don't place them right, and, brother, until I'm folded I'm going to be shooting."

Harry was on the floor, and he was living up to expectations. He was being sick. Homan stepped distastefully away from him. "I'm suprised at you, George," I said, still keeping my eyes on Pete. "Playing games with a hop-head! You know they're unreliable! You're a big boy now!"

"Who is this guy, George?" Pete asked, his eyes fastened on me. "He's no copper."

"Harry had a run-in with him this morning. I saw it, but the guy didn't see me. Harry popped off and this lug didn't like it. He's Kip Morgan."

That brought a gasp from the girl, but why, I couldn't guess. My eyes were on Pete, and I was realizing what I had not known before. Pete was top man here. Yet he was more than that to me. He was my life insurance.

"That's right, Pete," I said. "I'm Kip Morgan. If that name means anything to you at all you'll know I'm just the sort of damned fool who will shoot if you push me. Take that buzzard off the floor and back out of here. Back out fast."

Pete was watching me carefully. Pete was a smart guy. And he wasn't ready to die. Not yet.

"What if I say nothing doing?" he suggested. "What if we tell *you* to beat it?"

"Then don't waste time—just start shooting. I'll get George and Harry, Pete, but I'm getting you first. You're cold turkey and I'll lay you a thousand bucks to a dime I can blow a kidney right out your back from here."

"All right." I had guessed Pete would play it smart. I gambled on it. "We'll go, but we'll do a retake on this one. One thing I want to know. What's your angle? What are you nosing in for?"

"Sam Bradley was in my outfit overseas. He's a good guy and a good friend. Anything else?"

"Okay," Pete said, with a shrug. "You've proved you're a great big lovable boy. Now why don't you get smart and bow out? There's no percentage for you."

"I didn't come into this for laughs," I said. "When Sam Bradley is back home and in the clear, then I'll bow out. Until then, I'm in."

"What if I told you he was dead?" Pete said. "And his wife, too?"

That brought another gasp from the girl. I was wondering about her, and just where she belonged. "I wouldn't believe you unless I saw the bodies, and then I'd never rest until you three were either dead or standing in line for the gas chamber."

Pete smiled. "George," he said, "pick up Harry and sling his arm over your shoulder and get out to the car. I'll follow. This is no place or time to settle this."

Homan picked up Harry and turned for the door. Then he

looked over his shoulder at me. That look gave me a chill. I'd rather he had said something.

Pete started to follow them, keeping his eyes and gun on me. "You, too," I told the girl.

She started to protest. I cut her short. "Get going! Do you think I want you around to shoot me in the back? Get out, and, Pete, if you play it smart you'll have Sam and his wife back in their apartment before midnight. I'm giving you until then. After that I'm coming for you."

They went out the door, and the girl didn't look back. I felt sorry for her, but that might have been because she was pretty. She didn't look like a crook, but then . . . who does?

When they had gone I stood there staring at the door. I was still no closer to knowing what it was all about. Whatever it was, I knew that Sam Bradley, if not already dead, was in danger. If Pete was working with killers of the type of this Harry and George Homan, he was playing for keeps, and there had to be money in it, big money.

Before anything further could be done, I had to know what it was all about, and I had to find out who the girl was. Actually, had anyone asked me I'd have had no good reason for finding out what she was. She was apparently a gun moll, but she might be more, or less.

Come to think about it, I did have a clue. It was a flimsy one, certainly, but it was this girl's attitude toward Sam's Army friends. What had she meant by her remarks?

Right then I turned around and went to work to give that apartment a thorough shaking-down. In the writing desk I got my first good lead.

It was a circular, or rather a stack of them. Beside them, obviously for mailing, was a bunch of envelopes and a list of names, several of which I recognized as those of veterans I'd known or heard of.

Opening the circular, I glanced over it.

BOOM DAYS BOOM AGAIN!
Faro . . . Chuckaluck . . . Poker
Craps
Come one! Come all!
Proceeds to Wounded Veterans

Dropping into a chair I read the circular through and an idea began to germinate in my skull.

Where there is gambling there are sure-thing operators. They flock to money like bees to sugar, and unless I was much mistaken in the man, Pete was definitely a cinch player. Moreover, I had heard some comment lately about various professional gamblers moving in on veterans' games and taking them for considerable loot. They had probably spotted their own players through the crowds and were making a clean-up. Sam Bradley was on several veterans' committees.

Pete! . . . *Pete Merrano!* Owner of the Merrano Club! A bookie, a small-time racketeer who wanted to become big time, and a figure in the expanding numbers racket.

All I had was a hunch, but it was a good one. Supposing the vets had brought Merrano into the deal to operate their games, and supposing Merrano had been bleeding them and Bradley had discovered it? The idea no sooner took shape in my mind than I was sure I had the answer.

Now I had to get some evidence to back up my theory. Leaving the apartment, I went out by the service entrance and down the back stairs. Outside, I crossed the street and moved rapidly away. Once in my car I checked over the list of names I had carried away with me.

One, the name of Eugene Shidler, lived not far away. Starting my car I swung around the corner and headed down the street.

Shidler was at home. He came to the door in his shirt sleeves with a newspaper in his hand. He was a short, stocky man, partly bald. Showing him the leaflet, I asked what he knew about it.

"Only what all of us know. We wanted to raise some dough to give some of the boys a hand, and Earl Ramsey suggested a regular old-time gambling setup. It would last a week, sponsored by us. He said he knew just the man to handle it, that he had a lot of gambling equipment he had taken in on a loan, and that he was pretty sure he would provide the dealers, the equipment and the refreshment for a small cut of the proceeds.

"Naturally, it looked good to us. We would have to do nothing at all but come when the games started, and bring our friends. As we are all busy men, that was a big item. We had money, but very little time."

"Pete Merrano?"

"He's the one." Shidler looked at me thoughtfully. "What's the matter? Is there anything wrong?"

There seemed to be something underlying his question so I hesitated, then said slowly, "Yes, I think so. But first tell me how it all came out. Did you make money?"

"We cleared about a thousand dollars, although some of the boys figured it should have been more. In fact, there was a lot of talk about something crooked, but shucks, you know Sam as well as I do! There isn't a crooked bone in his body!"

"Yeah," I agreed, "that's right." I hesitated; then I broke down and told him. As much as I could, I gave him the whole story of what had happened, and told him that Bradley and his wife had vanished completely. "Merrano," I ended by saying, "hinted that Sam was dead. I don't believe that. Anyway, Merrano is worried about something, but just what I can't guess."

Shidler got to his feet. Angrily, he jerked his cigar from his mouth and stared at it with distaste. Glancing toward an inner door, he dropped suddenly on the sofa opposite me. "Look," he said, "if my wife hears of this I'll never know the last of it. I got rooked in that game, but plenty. They took me for five hundred bucks. I owe that much to Merrano."

"That makes sense, then," I said. "Merrano probably took the lot of you for plenty, and he's counting on you being good sports and keeping your mouths shut, or counting on you figuring it went to a good cause. Well, that cause was Pete Merrano's pocket. I'd bet money he took every one of you."

He nodded. "I lost about a hundred bucks in the games, then drifted into a side game that Pete was running. I lost forty more and finally ended by gambling on credit. Merrano holds my I.O.U. for five hundred now."

"Listen," I suggested, "get a few of the boys on the phone and do some checking. Tell them what the story is. Maybe we can get that money back. In the meantime, I'm going to find out about Sam Bradley."

It was after nine when I returned to my car. The best thing was to go to Mooney in the homicide squad and tell him the whole story. He knew me and would start the wheels going even though it lay outside his department. Although, I reflected, by this time it might not.

I decided, however, to do a little checking first. There was Earl Ramsey, who had recommended Merrano to handle the games, and was undoubtedly in with him. If Ramsey could be made to talk, the whole affair might be cleared up quickly. And before everything else I must think of Sam and Ellen.

It seemed strange to be riding down a brightly lighted street, with all about me people going their way to or from home, to the theatre or to dinner, and to realize that somewhere in all these thousands upon thousands of buildings a man and his wife were in danger. That even now they might be facing death. Yet without evidence, I could do nothing, and there was that hunch I'd had earlier that made me doubt they had been killed.

Checking the list, I found Ramsey's name. The address was some distance off but worth a visit. If Ramsey were not tied in with the crooks, he might talk.

It was a large, old-fashioned frame house on a corner near a laundry. Parking the car I got out and went up the steps. There was a light in one of the rear rooms, so I pressed the bell. Three times I rang with no response, and then I saw the door was not quite closed. It was open, but no more than a crack.

Had it been closed when I came up? The impression persisted that it had. That meant someone had softly opened it even as I stood there! An eerie feeling went over me and I shifted my feet restlessly, trying the bell again and suddenly wishing the street were not so dark.

For the second time that day I pushed open a door I had no business to touch. It swung open and I stared into the darkness of a large living room that seemed a veritable cavern where anything might lurk. "Hello!" I called out. "Mr. Ramsey?"

Silence, and through it a subdued whispering, but not of voices, a whispering of surreptitious movement.

A clock ticked solemnly, and somewhere I could hear water running in a basin. Uncomfortably, I looked around. The street was dark and empty except for my own car and another that was parked in darkness farther down the street. Frowning, and momentarily distracted from the house, I stared at that car. I hadn't noticed it when I first came up.

Suddenly a hand reached out of the darkness and grasped my arm.

I jumped. Then for a long moment I stood there absolutely motionless, afraid to trust my voice. I started to pull my hand away, but the grasp tightened and a voice came from the shadows, a voice so old you could hear the wrinkles in it. "Come in, won't you? Did you wish to see Earl?"

It was an old woman's voice, but there was something else in it that set my nerves on edge, and I'm not easily bothered.

"Yes, I want to see him. Is he in?"

"He's in the kitchen. He came home to eat and I put out a lunch for him. Maybe you would like something? A cup of coffee?"

The house was too warm and the air was close and stuffy. She walked ahead of me toward a dim rectangle of doorway. "Just follow me. I never use the lights, but Earl likes them."

She led the way down a bare hall and I saw a door framed with a thread of light. When she opened that door I saw Earl Ramsey.

He was seated at a kitchen table, his chin propped on his hand, the other hand against the side of his face. There was a cup before him and an untasted sandwich on his plate. He was staring at me as I came through the door.

"Hello, are you Ramsey?" I said.

He neither spoke nor blinked, and I stepped past the old woman and stopped flat-footed with cold chills going down my spine. I was looking into the eyes of a dead man.

Turning, overcome with horror, I stared at the old woman who had begun puttering among some dirty dishes. "Don't mind him," she said. "Earl was never one for talking much. Only when he takes the notion."

My skin crawled. She turned her head and looked at me and her eyes were blank and expressionless. Grey hair straggled about a face that looked old enough to have worn out two bodies, and her clothing was misshapen and soiled. She fumbled at her pocket, staring at me.

It gave me the creeps. The hot, stuffy air and this aged and obviously imbecilic woman and her dead son.

Then I stepped past the table and saw the knife. It had been driven into the left side of his back, driven up from below as he sat at the table, and driven to the hilt. I touched the hand of Earl Ramsey. It was cold.

The old woman was puttering among the dishes, unaware and unconcerned. "Have you a telephone in the house?" I asked.

She neither stopped nor heard me, so I stepped past her to the hallway and found a switch. Turning it on, I saw a telephone standing on a small table in the corner. It took me only a minute to get Mooney. "Mooney? Morgan here." I gave him the address. "This is a funny one. Can you come right over? . . . Dead? Sure, he's dead! Yes, I'll wait."

Walking back into the kitchen, I looked around, but there was nothing that might have been a clue. Nothing I could see, but then, I wasn't a cop. Only, I was willing to bet the killer had come in the door behind Ramsey and that he had probably dropped a hand on his shoulder and then slammed the knife home. And the shiv? From the look of the hilt it was a dead ringer for the one I'd taken from Harry only that morning.

CHAPTER THREE

Dead Man's Tide

Several steps led down from that open door behind Ramsey to a small landing. It was dark down there, and a door opened outside that probably would let a man out on the narrow space between the house and the laundry next door. I went down the steep steps and grasped the knob to see for myself.

There was a whisper of movement in the darkness of the corner behind me and I started to turn. Then something smashed down over my skull, and my legs folded under me. And I fell, my arm swept out and grabbed a man around the knees. There was a nasty oath and another blow smashed the last vestige of consciousness from me. Then I seemed to be falling down a steep slide into engulfing blackness.

Yet even as consciousness faded I heard a tearing of cloth and somewhere, far away, the sound of a police siren, wild and anxious.

When next I became aware of anything I was lying on a damp, hard floor in absolute darkness. Fear washed over me in a cold wave, and with a lunge I heaved myself to a sitting position. My head swam with pain at the sudden movement and I put both my hands to it, finding a laceration across my scalp from one of the blows. My hair was matted with blood. I got to my knees finally, but I was shaky and my thoughts refused to become coherent.

All the events of the night were in a jumble now—the hot, close air of the kitchen and the hallway, the dead man, the weird old woman, and the sudden blows in the entranceway.

Somehow I had stumbled into something uglier than I had expected. A man had been murdered. Perhaps Bradley, too, was dead.

Feeling for my shoulder holster I found my gun was gone. That was to be expected. The floor on which I stood was concrete, and there was no light. The room had a dank, musty smell, and the thought came to me that I must be in the basement of the murder house. Then I placed another smell, one that I knew. It was the smell of the sea.

Then I had been taken from the house and dumped here. Why? Had they believed me dead? Or had they lacked time to kill me?

Four steps and I touched a wall. Feeling my way cautiously along the wall, I found three stone steps and at the top, a door. Carefully testing and examining the door, I found no knob or latch, not even a hinge. Nor was there a finger hold anywhere. The door was fitted with admirable precision.

Working cautiously, then, I circled the room, keeping my hands on the wall. The room was about ten feet wide by twenty long and appeared to be empty, although I had not been down the center of it. At the far end there was an opening in the wall almost on the floor level It was perhaps three feet wide and covered with a grating of iron bars. They were not heavy, but definitely beyond the power of my unaided muscles. Dropping to my knees I peered out, and in the distance I could see a faint line of greyness some distance off and below the level of the floor. My fingers encountered damp sand about the grate.

Fumbling in my pockets for a cigarette I found nothing had

been left me. They had carefully removed all my belongings and even, I found, the labels from inside my coat. That meant one thing. I was marked for murder.

The pieces began to fall into place and as each one fitted into place I felt a mounting horror and fear. The grate near the floor . . . the smell of the sea . . . that damp sand *inside* the window . . . the faint line of grey! *At high tide this place was under water!*

I rushed across the room and hurled myself at the door, grabbing and tearing at the edges, but nowhere could I get a handhold, and it was of heavy planks, a door made to stay where it was placed. In all probability, a water-tight door!

I shouted and pounded, but there was no sound. Pausing, gasping for breath, sweat trickling down my face and body, I listened. All was vast and empty silence, the silence of complete nothingness. I was alone then. Alone in a deserted place with no chance of outside help. And then, very slightly at first, I heard a sound. It was a faint, rustling sound, ever so soft, ever so distant. It was the sea. The tide was coming in.

Thinking about it, I began to realize that they had known I was alive. They had left me here to be drowned by the inflowing water, probably still unconscious. Then they could dispose of my body, and as it would carry all the evidences of drowning, it would be passed off as suicide.

Whoever the killers were, they had evidently returned to Earl Ramsey's house to find me there, and when I walked into their hands they had slugged me, then dumped me here. That car parked outside in the dark must have been the car they came in, and the car in which I had been taken away.

Yet I had called Mooney first, and Mooney would know that something had gone wrong when I was not among those present after telling him I would be.

For the first time in my life I found myself in a spot that seemed to offer no solution. How high the tide would rise in this room I could not guess. Nor did I know how high the tide usually rose along this coast. That it would be high enough to drown me I didn't doubt.

They had taken my matches and my lighter. Seated on the steps I tried to puzzle it out, searching my mind for a way to get past that grate. Yet even as I sat there, the room seemed to have grown lighter, and for several minutes the cause did not occur to me. Then I realized that the tide was rising, and the added light, little as it was, was reflected from the nearing water.

It was only a faint grey light, but on my knees by the grate I could peer out and see that the opening was under a wharf or dock, and beyond a short stretch of sandy beach was the lapping water of the incoming tide.

Crossing the room through the middle I saw something dangling from the beams overhead that I'd not seen before. Staring at it, I moved closer, then put out a tentative hand. It was a chain. A double chain. I pulled on it and heard it rattle on a block.

A chain hoist!

This basement room must have been used to overhaul something heavy. Boat engines, probably. Running my hand down the chain I found the hook, and suddenly my heart was pounding with excitement. The chance was a wild one, an absurd one, actually. Yet a chance was a chance.

I hauled the chain hook over to the grate. Hooking it around one of the bars, I hauled the chain tight. Even as I tightened my grip on the chain and heaved my weight on it, I knew the chance of pulling the grate loose was pitifully small. But I was in no position to pass up anything. My weight is a muscular two hundred pounds, and I gave a hard heave. The grate held. I tried again and again, hoping that the action of the sea water, certain to have weakened the concrete in which the bars were set, would have weakened them enough.

No luck. Panting, my shirt wet with perspiration, I stopped and mopped my face. The water was almost to the edge of the window now. It meant nothing that the water might not rise high enough. If they came back and found me here my goose was cooked anyway. I tried again, then gave up the chance as useless. My luck was damned poor.

I studied the concrete in which the grate was set. There seemed little enough to hold it in place, but it was too much for my strength. With a sledge hammer, now—but I had no sledge hammer, or anything like it. Moreover, as the grate was set inside, the force would have to be applied from the outside. And there was no chance of that. It was useless to consider it.

Or was it? Suddenly, I saw something long and black bobbing upon the water outside the window. It was some distance away, but at each movement of the tide it drew nearer. At first it looked like the body of a man. Then I saw it was a timber, all of six feet long, and about a six by six.

The water moved in, lapped at the sill below the grate, then retreated. Then it moved nearer, and each time the beam came closer.

I dashed back to the center of the room and, gathering the chains in my hands, pulled myself high enough to release the catch. Then dropping back to the floor, I flipped the chain out of the block and made a loop of it. I pushed the loop through the grate—and waited.

The beam moved closer, and I tried to snag it with the chain, but without luck. Again and again I tried to grasp it, and failed. Sweat poured down my face and body. I fought desperately, working with the patience of fear and desperation to catch the end of that timber.

Twice, I almost had it in the loop of the chain, but each time it slipped free. Then the tide brought it close again. This time it actually bumped the sill below the grate, and I grabbed it with both hands. The water retreated, but I had beached the timber, and after a few minutes of struggle I had a half hitch around the end. If this trick did not work, then I was finished.

Roughly as I could estimate my chances, I had about thirty minutes, perhaps less, in which to work. If by that time I was not successful then the water would have risen so high that I could do no more.

The waves returned, and this time a little water spilled over the sill. I gathered the chain in my hands, and when next the waves started I heaved in with all my strength on the chain. The butt of the timber came crashing against the grate. I relaxed, then heaved again. The waves retreated a little and I waited for them to return. This time I got in three smashing blows at the grate with my crude battering ram before the water rolled back. By now there was always some water over the sill, and it was on the floor about my feet.

As the minutes passed I battered at the grate. My muscles began to ache and I was panting, hoarsely, but I worked on. Once something seemed to give, and I bent over the grate, putting out trembling fingers. My pulse gave a leap. The bars at one side of the window were broken free.

Letting go of the chain, but anchoring it with a foot, I seized the bars in my two hands and gave a tremendous heave. Again and again I lunged back, and little by little they bent inward. When I had space enough, I got my hands down through the opening and grabbed the timber. I worked and pulled until I had it through the opening I'd made. Then, using the butt end of it as a sledge, I took the timber and battered the grate back until there was opening enough for me to slip through.

Gasping heavily, I went through, scrambled to my feet and splashed through the knee-deep water toward the dim outline of a ladder. I crawled up and only when sprawled at full length on the dock did I relax.

It was there she found me.

How long I had been sprawled there I do not know, but it could have been no more than a few minutes. Then I heard a car motor and something snapped my eyes wide open. A car meant danger. The next thing I knew heels were clicking on the dock and I came to my feet with a lunge. Drunk with fatigue, I stood there, poised for battle.

It was the girl, the girl I had met in Sam's apartment. When she saw me, she stopped running. "Oh! You're free! You're safe!"

That stopped me all right. "You bet I'm free," I said, staring at her. "But it isn't your fault or that of your friends."

"They aren't my friends," she protested. "It wasn't until a few minutes ago that someone dropped a remark so that I found out where you were. I knew they had you somewhere, but I didn't know where."

"What about Bradley?" I demanded. "What about his wife?"

"We haven't found them," she replied. "Nobody seems to know where they are."

"I'll bet your friend Merrano knows!"

She looked at me, her eyes puzzled. "He might," she admitted. "He acts funny about her. He's looking for Sam, I know."

I had no reason to trust her and did not. However, she had a car. "Let's get started for town," I said. "I've got to get some clothes."

She handed me a gun. "It's yours. I stole it back from them."

That didn't make sense. Not any way I looked at it. One minute she was with them and sticking me up at gunpoint, and the next she was giving me a gun. I checked the clip. It was loaded, all right.

"How did I rate this trip of yours?" I asked. "Did you come out to see if I was dead yet?"

"Oh, be still!" she said impatiently. "We're on the same side!" She looked at me quickly then. "I'd better tell you my name. It's Pat Mulrennan."

"That's nice," I said. "That's ducky. Now we're all introduced and we can speak, or maybe even hold hands. Well, honey, I'm still not turning my back on you."

She sounded honest and possibly she was, but nothing about the setup looked good to me. That is, except her. She looked as if she was shaped to order to keep me awake nights thinking about her, but I couldn't forget how chummy she had been with Pete Merrano and Harry, to say nothing of that big-time torpedo, George Horman.

"To be honest," Pat said, "I wasn't sure you were here, but from a remark I heard I thought you might be, and I knew that Pete had been using this place for something. How I'd get you out, I didn't know, but I came, anyway. Then as I got out of my car I saw something or someone lying out there on the dock."

There was nothing I could think of to say, so just kept still, running my mind over the whole setup and trying to figure where Neal could be.

"You were closer to being killed than you dreamed," she said. "The police had a running gunfight with the car you were in. They ditched the car and switched you to another one."

At my apartment I tried to call Sam, never taking my eyes off Pat. I'll say this for her. I didn't trust her but she was easy to watch. In fact, I was beginning to like it. "If you're so friendly," I said, hanging up, "why not tell me where Sam is?"

"I don't know." She sounded sincere. "Look, please forget all that this morning. I didn't know you were a friend of Sam's. For all I knew you were somebody trying to cut in on Pete's deal."

"And you were fronting for Pete?" I asked.

"No, I wasn't. I was with him, but I had a job of my own to do. He means nothing to me."

She finished saying it and then Pete was standing there in the door to my bedroom. He was standing there with a gun in his hand and this time mine was still in my holster. Where he had come from I could guess, for there was a fire escape right outside my window. A moment before I had been in the bedroom, picking up a clean shirt, but I had not seen him then.

"Is that so?" Pete asked. He was looking at me but he was talking to Pat. "So I mean nothing to you? All right, chick, have it your way. You mean nothing to me, then. When this lad goes out you can go with him."

Not for a second did his eyes flicker off mine, and, believe me, I was doing some fast thinking. "This is no place for a bump-off, Pete," I said quietly. "There's too many people around. You'd have them all down your neck in no time."

He didn't smile: he didn't change expression. "What if I use a shiv? What if I borrow a note from Harry?" He chuckled. "Why, they might even think Harry did it. I heard they're fingering him for that Ramsey killing."

"So that's it," I said. "You let your boys take the raps."

"Why not? Why have killers around unless they're some good to me? I do my own killing, but everybody knows what Harry and George are like. Naturally they'd get the blame."

"You're probably right," I agreed, "and you've played this one smart except for one thing: How did Sam get away with the money?"

That was a guess, nothing but a guess, although that was the only reason I could really think of for him to be so anxious to get hold of Bradley. Also, if my guess was wrong, I figured to learn so from what he said.

"How do you know he's got the money?" His eyes sharpened

and he studied me more carefully. "Say," he said suspiciously, "do you know where he is? Where the money is?"

"Why would I be looking for him if I did?" I asked, shrugging that one off. "Anyway, even if I did I wouldn't talk, as things stand."

"No?" Somehow, despite the way they had made their killing, Sam Bradley had laid hands on the money. No wonder they wanted him. "Will you tell me where he is if I turn you and the babe loose?"

"Suppose you do?" I shrugged. "That isn't enough."

"Suppose, then," he asked carefully, "I turn Ellen loose, too? I've been hanging onto her but haven't been able to let Bradley know I've got her."

Another point cleared up, but doubt seemed to come into his mind. "That's enough talk," he said. "How do I know you know anything? Turn around!" His voice was low and deadly. I turned.

CHAPTER FOUR

Violent Visitor

It was still early, and in a matter of minutes the milkman would be coming around. "Look," I said, "Mooney was to meet me here in a few minutes. I just called him."

Gambling that he had seen me on the phone, I hoped the bluff might work. He had probably seen me, and I knew from experience that even in the bedroom one could not hear what was said over the phone if the speaker did not deliberately talk loud.

"You wouldn't tell me that if he was really coming," he said, but there was doubt in his voice.

"Be your age, Pete," I said. "Do you suppose I want you guys swapping bullets, with me in the middle? You had better lam while you can. But," I added, "you turn Ellen loose and I'll see you get the money."

"Yeah?" he sneered. "What's she to you?"

My answer came fast, and I lied. "She's my sister, you dope!"

That made sense to him. "All right," he said. "But get this: She's being watched by George Homan. He has orders to kill her if he's approached. If the police find her, he'll knock her off and blow out. We've got a getaway all set."

"What about your club?"

He laughed. "I owe money on it. There's nearly fifteen grand in that bag Bradley has."

He moved back of me. I could hear him, and from the bedroom door he said, "All right, you get the dough and call me at home. I'll tell you where to meet me. You've got until noon. This thing is too hot for comfort."

Merrano turned Pat around too, and we both stood there facing the wall. I counted a slow one hundred, giving him time to get clear. Then I lowered my hands a little, and when nothing was said, I put them all the way down and turned. The bedroom door was empty, and when I looked, Pete was gone. A check showed that he must have been on the fire escape when I came in. He had been through the closet and had given the apartment a thorough shaking-down.

For a few minutes I stood there thinking it over. Pete Merrano was worried. His big plan to clean up a lot of money had flopped on him when somehow Bradley had gotten away with the money. He had put the snatch on Ellen but had not been able to get in touch with Sam to use that as a selling point. Then I had barged into the deal and, as usual, had messed things up by kicking around in all the wrong places. Evidently Ramsey had cold feet and they had killed him when he wanted to duck out. At least, so I had it figured.

Now the next question was what to do? I'd made a promise I could not back up, for I had no idea where Sam was, and I was positive Pete had been telling the truth when he said that Homan was watching Ellen. That left the situation exceedingly shaky. Yet, there was a way.

"Look, Pat," I said. "I'm going to trust you. You go to Mooney and tell him what happened. Tell him I'm following my inclinations, and he'll know what the score is. He'll also know what to do." Knowing Mooney, I could bet on that. Pat, not knowing him, or so I believed, would make nothing of what I had said.

She looked at me. "All right," she said, "but you be careful. Those boys aren't playing for fun."

She was telling *me?*

We parted there, and I glanced back over my shoulder at her and her eyes were wide as she watched me go. For a minute I thought she actually looked worried, but that would not make sense. So I went out, and around the corner I hailed a cab. My own car was still near Ramsey's, for all I knew, and where I was going a cab would be better. I started in walking.

Peter Merrano had been doing all right for himself. He lived in a picturesque ranch house overlooking the Strip, and I left the cab a few doors away and walked on up the hill. Skirting the fence I walked toward a rear gate and glimpsed a Filipino boy wearing a white jacket coming down the steps from the back door. He turned on the sprinkler to water the lawn and then walked around the house. As soon as his back was turned I went through that back gate and up the steps and into the back door.

There was a pot of coffee on the stove, so I picked up a cup and poured it full. Taking a swallow, I started up the hall with the cup still in my left hand.

Harry was snoring on a divan in the living room, and Pete was sprawled across a bed, with only his tie and shoes off, in a bedroom. I sat down and finished my coffee, then lit a smoke. By that time I knew just what I was going to do.

The houseboy was working around in the yard, so I got up, cut a length of cord from the Venetian blinds and, working very cautiously, slid the end under Harry's ankles. Then I drew it as tight as I dared and tied it.

His gun was lying on the floor with his shoulder holster and I slid it under the divan and out of sight. Picking up his handkerchief I placed it within easy reach, and then very gently I lifted one of his wrists and laid it over his stomach. I'd just lifted the second one to bring it into tying position when he opened his eyes.

By his breath and the bottle nearby, I could tell he had taken more than a few drinks before he passed out on the divan, and his awakening wasn't pleasant for him. He opened his eyes to find a man bending over him who he had every reason to believe was dead or dying.

For one startled instant Harry stared up at me while his thoughts came into focus, and then he started up, opening his mouth to yell. That instant was all I needed, and as his mouth popped open I jammed the handkerchief into it. He choked, grabbing at my wrists, but I jerked a hand free and slugged him in the windpipe. Then, grabbing him by the pants at the hips, I jerked him up and flopped him over on his face.

He struggled, but he was at least fifty pounds lighter than I, and in neither the condition nor the place to put up much of a fight. With my knee in his back and his face muffled in the pillow, I got his hands behind him and got a slip knot over one wrist, then a turn around the other. In less than a minute his hands were tied, and then I gagged him.

Pete's voice sounded from the bedroom and jerked me upright with gooseflesh running up my spine. "Hey! You sick again, Harry? For the luvva Mike, beat it for the bathroom! That carpet's worth a fortune!"

I took my knee out of Harry's back and started toward the bedroom, keeping out of line of sight from the doorway. Merrano evidently listened a minute, and then I heard him muttering to himself. The bedsprings creaked as he got up and I heard his feet feeling for his slippers. Right then I was thinking of Sam and Ellen and the way he had tried to murder me by drowning. There was no mercy in me.

Merrano came through the door scratching his stomach and blinking, and I never gave him a chance. Grabbing him by his shirt sleeve I spun him toward me and hooked one into his belly. The blow was wicked and unexpected, and his mouth went wide as he grabbed for air. As he doubled up I slapped one hand to the back of his head and jerked his face down to meet my upcoming knee.

That straightened him up again and he staggered, blood all over his face, and with one hand clawing for the gun in his hip pocket, I ignored the reaching hand and stepped closer, throwing two punches, short and hard to the chin. His knees melted under him and he hit the floor. Reaching over, I slid the rod from his pocket to my own, then jerked him to his feet.

He wasn't out, but he had neither the wind to yell with nor the opportunity. Grabbing him by the shirt collar I stood him on his toes. "All right, bud, you wanted to play rough. You started bouncing me around. Now where's Ellen Bradley?"

He gasped for a minute, and the blood running from his broken nose splashed on my wrist. There had been no chance for him to assemble his thoughts. Pete Merrano was like all his kind—they live by fear and terror, and when that fails them, they're backed in a corner. He had been so sure he was going to win. He had been sure when everything went against him, for he still believed he was too smart. He had forgotten the old adage that the cops can make many mistakes, but a crook only one.

Pete Merrano had made several, and now it was dawning on him that all people didn't scare.

"Where is she?" I persisted.

He shook his head. "Try and find out!"

This was no time to play, so I slugged him in the belly again and tightened my grip on his collar. "Look, Bad Boy, you're making me sore. If that girl is harmed in any way at all, the gas chamber will be a picnic to what I'll give you. Where is she?"

He glared at me, and his eyes were insane with fury. "You'd like to know, wouldn't you? You think you can make me talk? Why, you . . .!"

He jerked away from me and I let him go. Then he swung. It was a roundhouse right and I stepped inside of it and hit him with both hands. The punches I'd slammed him with before had been kitten blows compared to these. The first one smashed his lips into his teeth and the second lifted his feet right out of his slippers. He hit the floor as if he'd been dropped off a roof. Jerking him to his feet, I showed him against the wall and began slapping him. I slapped him over and back, keeping my head inside of his futile swings, and slapped him until his head must have been buzzing like a sawmill.

When I let up, there was desperation in his eyes. "How does it feel to be on the wrong end of a slugging?" I asked him. "You dish it out, but you can't take it. Now where is she? I don't like crooks. I don't like double-crossers. And I especially don't like crooks who pick on women. I'm in good shape and I'm getting sore, so I can keep this up all day. Three or four hours of it will get mighty tiresome.''

He just stared at me, and I've never seen such hatred in a man's eyes. Then there was something else, and I knew that he'd had an idea. "She's at the club," he said, "but you'll never get her. You find Bradley and get the money and we'll turn her loose.''

Shoving him back on the bed I grabbed his coat and threw it to him. "Get into that. You're coming with me.''

Merrano did not like that. He didn't like it even a little bit, but I'd slipped my gun into my hand and he got into his coat, and I started him for the door. He stared at Harry, still lying on the divan, as I hurried him out into the street.

We stopped the car a short distance from the club. There was nobody in sight. It was too early for the bar to open, and so I kept the gun in my pocket while Pete fiddled with his keys and opened the door.

It was all I could do to keep my eyes open. My muscles felt heavy and I was dead tired. The long fight to escape from that cellar was taking it out of me now when the strain was easing up a little. If Ellen was actually here Homan would be watching her. That, I believed, was what Merrano was counting on. He was planning on me walking into Homan, and both of us knew what that meant, for George would ask no questions. He was trigger-happy and kill-crazy. Nor, I decided, would Merrano's presence stop him. If he figured he was due for a pinch he would mow Pete down to get me.

We started across the polished floor. It was shadowed and cool in here, the tables stacked with chairs, and the piano ghostly in the vague light. We headed toward a door that led backstage from the orchestra stand. Pete went through the door ahead of me, and then I heard a girl scream. I sprang aside—but not quite enough, for I caught a ringing blow on the side of the head from a blackjack. George Homan had been waiting right beside the door.

My .45 blasted a hole in the ceiling as I went down, but I was only stunned and shaken by the blow, not knocked out. Scrambling to my feet I was just in time to see Homan, his eyes blazing like a madman's, cutting down on me with a sawed-off shotgun.

That was one time I shot before I thought. That shotgun and his eyes were like a trigger in my tired brain, and I blasted at him with three fast shots. Somewhere another shot rang out even as my first one sounded. I saw him jerk as the first bullet hit him, smashing his right hand and wrist, going through into his body. The second two shots hit him from my gun as he was falling. The other shot had come from a side door, or somewhere.

Leaping over him, I started after Pete Merrano. Ellen Bradley was tied to a chair in the office, and Merrano was grabbing for a desk drawer behind her. I lunged through the door and Pete got his gun, but he elected not to fight it out and dove through another door in the corner behind some filing cabinets. He feet clattered on a stair and I jumped past Ellen and started after him.

There were a dozen steps leading down to a street door and he wheeled at the door and fired at me, but his shot was taken too quickly and missed me by two feet, striking the door jamb over my head. Then I fired and he jerked open the door and went out. There was a shot outside, then a rattle of gunfire followed by a silence.

Standing there with my Colt gripped in my fist, I waited, wondering what had happened and hesitant to leave Ellen. Then the door was blocked by a shadow and Mooney stepped into sight. "Put it away, Kip," he said. "Merrano ran into the boys. He's through."

"How did you get here?" I demanded. "You're the last guy I expected to see!"

Two more men came through the door and with them was Pat Mulrennan. We stared at each other, and I thought I saw a flash of relief on her face but couldn't be sure. "I see you got her," I said. "Where does she fit in?"

Mooney grinned at me. "This is Sergeant Patricia Mulrennan," he said. "She's been working undercover for us. She knew Ellen Bradley, all right, so it worked out fine."

While he was speaking I stepped over and began untying Ellen. Before I could finish, Sam Bradley brushed by me and took the job out of my hands. In a minute they were in each other's arms and both of them either laughing or crying. We walked outside.

"You were already on this case? You knew about Merrano?"

"Sure, but we had no evidence. We knew what was going on, but we couldn't get our hands on anything. It was your tip on the Ramsey killing that gave us a break. He was a small-time crook, not right in the head, and he started by being the man who led Merrano into these jobs. Nobody in the service groups knew him as anything but a quiet sort of guy, and that's all he was, usually. But he had done time and he worked with Pete Merrano on small jobs. When Pete put the snatch on Ellen Bradley, however, he got cold feet and was going to talk to us. So they killed him.

"Naturally, that gave us a direct lead, because we knew who he worked with. They killed him, but they knew he had written a letter to the D.A. containing the whole story, and they came back after it. That is, they didn't know it when they killed him, but Ramsey had told one of the others what he meant to do, and Pete came back after the letter and ran into you."

Mooney grinned. "You had a close shave in that car. We picked it up in Redondo shot full of holes."

"You lost us?"

"Yeah, and in the meantime Bradley found out his wife wasn't with her sister as he had believed. So he came to us. That filled in the rest of it, and after you left Pat Mulrennan this morning we knew the whole story."

Then I remembered Harry, and explained quickly. Mooney ducked out to send after him, and Ellen Bradley came to me. "Thanks, Kip. Sam told me all you've done."

Mooney had just come back and Pat was standing there when the door opened and Edward Pollard walked in. He had taken three fast steps before he saw Mooney and the cops. The police cars were mostly around at the other door, and we had moved on into the main room.

He stopped abruptly. From where I was standing with Ellen and Pat, I couldn't be seen so easily, and his eyes were on Mooney and the cops.

"I guess I'm a bit late, Lieutenant," he said smoothly, "or is Mr. Merrano in? He asked me to represent him in a criminal case."

"Merrano?" Mooney studied Pollard thoughtfully. "No, he's out of trouble. He's out of trouble for good."

"Oh, I'm sorry. Well, nothing for me, then. I'll be going. Good-morning."

He turned, but as he turned I was moving. That briefcase in Pollard's hands had suddenly begun to seem awfully big to the lawyer, I could see that. He was walking rapidly for the front door when I ducked past Mooney and started for the side door. I went out running and made the car just as Pollard did.

Mooney and the others had followed, and stopped on the walk behind Pollard.

"Take your hand off my car door," Pollard said. "I've no time to waste."

"No, you haven't, Ed," I told him, "not now. But in a few weeks you'll have plenty of time. You'll be doing time."

"I don't know what you're talking about," he said.

"I've still got the card you left at Bradley's place, Ed. You wanted him to come down here and walk right into a trap. That card should help convict you, but I've a hunch we'll find more in that briefcase."

His eyes were desperate now. "Get out of my way!" he said viciously.

Mooney had come up behind him. "Maybe we'd better have a look at the briefcase," he said quietly.

All the spirit went out of Pollard. His face turned grey and old and he turned on Mooney. "Let me go." His voice sank to a whisper. "Let me go, Lieutenant. I'll pay. I'll pay plenty."

Mooney had opened the briefcase and was shuffling through the papers. "You should have thought of that before you started to help gyp a lot of vets out of their money." He glanced up sharply at me. "Morgan, I don't know how you do it, but unless I miss my guess you've stumbled into the man who engineered the whole thing. From the look of this stuff he must have been coming to settle up with Merrano."

"Look," I said, "you work that out anyway you like. I'm going to buy Pat a drink and then I'm going home and sleep for a week!"

We'd made three steps before Mooney called out. "You'd better watch that guy, Pat. He's a good man in the clinches!"

Pat laughed and we kept going. In the clinches, I had an idea Pat could take care of herself.

STREET OF LOST CORPSES

CHAPTER ONE

The Shadow in the Hallway

In a shabby room in a dingy hotel on a street of pawn shops, cheap night clubs and sour-smelling bars, a man sat on a hard chair and stared at a collection of odds and ends scattered on the bed before him. There was no sound in the room but the low mutter of a small electric fan which threw an impotent stream of air against his chest and shoulders.

He was a big man, powerfully built, yet lean in the hips and waist. His shoes were off and his shirt hung over the foot of the bed. It was hot in the room despite the two open windows, and from time to time he mopped his face and chest with a towel.

The bed was ancient, the wash bowl rust stained, the bedspread ragged. Here and there the wall paper had begun to peel, and the door fitted badly. Again, for the forty-ninth time, the man ran his fingers through a shock of dark, unruly hair and swore softly.

Before him lay the puzzle of the odd pieces. Four news clippings, a torn bit of paper on which was written all or part of a number, and a crumpled pawn ticket. He stared at them gloomily and muttered at the heat. It was hot, hotter than it had any right to be in Los Angeles.

Occupied though he was, he did not fail to hear the click of heels in the hall outside, or the soft tap on the door. He slid from his chair, swift and soundless as a big cat, and in his hand there was a flat, ugly Colt .38 automatic.

Again the tap sounded. Turning the key in the lock, he stepped back from the door. "Who is it?" he asked, his voice low.

"It's me." The voice was low, husky, feminine. "May I come in?"

He drew back, shoving the gun into his waistband. "Sure. Sure, come on in."

She was neat, neat as a new dime, and nothing about the way

she was dressed left anything to the imagination. Moreover, her blouse was cheap and the skirt cheaper. She wore too much mascara and too much rouge and much too much lipstick. Her hose were very sheer and her heels too high.

He waved her to a chair, but his eyes were cold. "At least you had sense enough to look the part. Didn't I tell you to stay away from me?"

His voice was purposely low, for the walls were thin. "I had to come!" She stepped closer, and despite the heat and the cheapness of her makeup he felt the shock of her nearness and drew back. "I've been frightened and worried. You must know how worried I am! Have you learned anything?"

"Shut up!" His voice was ugly. "Now listen to me. I took the job of finding your brother, and if he's alive, I'll find him. If he's dead, I'll find out what happened to him. In the meantime, stay away from me and leave me alone! Remember what happened to that other dick."

"But you've no reason to believe they killed him for this investigation," she protested. "Why would they? You told me yourself he had enemies."

"Sure, he had enemies. He was a fast operator and a shrewd one. Nevertheless, he'd been around a long time and was still alive. As to why they should kill him for looking into this job, I don't know. All I know is that anything can happen down here, and everything *has* happened at one time or another. I don't know what happened to your brother or why a dick should get a knife stuck into him for trying to find out. Until I do know, I'm being careful."

"It's been over a week," she protested. "I had to know something. Tell me what you've found out and I'll go!"

"You'll stay right here," he said disagreeably, "until I tell you to go. You came of your own accord—now you'll go when I tell you to go. You'll stay for at least an hour, long enough to make them think you're my girl and you came for that reason. You look the part—now act it!"

"Just what do you expect?" she demanded icily.

"Listen," he said. "I'm just talking about the looks of the thing. I'm working, not playing. You've put me on the spot by

coming here, as I'm not supposed to know anybody around town.
Now sit down and stay a while, and if you hear anybody in the
hall, make with the soft talk, get me?"

She shrugged. "All right, I'll do my part." She shook out a
cigarette, then offered him one. He shook his head impatiently,
and she stared at him, irritated. "I wonder if you're as tough as
you act?"

"You'd better hope I am," he said dryly, "or you may have
another stiff on your hands."

He stared grimly at the collection on the bed, and Marilyn
Marcy stared at him. Some, she reflected, would call him
handsome, and men would turn to look at him because of his
shoulders and that toughness that made him look as if he carried
a permanent chip on his shoulder. Women would look, then turn
to look again. She had seen them do it.

"Look," he said suddenly. "Let's face it. Your brother was
an alcoholic. He was on the skids and on them bad, and we may
not find him alive."

Her lips were thin now. "I realize that, but I must know. I
loved my brother, despite his faults, and I must know what
happened to him. Aside from George, he was all I had in this
world.

"We loved each other and we understood each other, and
either of us would do anything to help the other. He was always
weak, and both of us knew it. Yet when he went into the Army
he was a fairly normal man. He simply wasn't up to it, and when
he received word that his wife had left him, it broke him up.

"However," she added, "this much I know. If my brother is
dead it was not suicide. It would have to be accident or murder.
If it was the former, I want to know how and why, and if
the latter, I want the murderer brought to trial."

He searched her face as he listened. Having seen her without
makeup he knew she was a beautiful girl, and even before she
hired him he had seen her on the stage, many times. "You seem
ready to accept the idea of murder. Why should anyone want to
kill your brother?"

"I've heard they kill for very little down here."

He nodded. "They do, all right. In a flophouse up the street
there was a man killed for thirty-five cents once. Value, you

know, is a matter of comparison. A dollar may seem very little, but if you don't have one, and want it badly, it can mean as much as a thousand."

"I know," she said. "I've seen the time." Drawing her purse nearer, she drew out some bills and counted out ten fives. "You will need expense money," she said. "If you need more, let me know."

His attention returned to the collection on the bed. The answer had to be there. "Did Tom ever say anything about quitting the bottle? Or show any desire to?"

"No, never. I've told you how he was fixed. Each month he received a certain sum of money from me. We always met in a cheap restaurant on a street where neither of us ever went except at the time when he was to receive the money from me. Tom was eager to keep anyone from knowing that he was my brother, for he believed himself a disgrace to me. He had enough from me to buy what he neded and to live with some small comfort. He could have had more, but he wouldn't accept it."

Morgan nodded, then looked up. "What would you say," he suggested, "if I told you that for three weeks prior to his disappearance he hadn't touched a drop?"

Her eyes were doubting. "How can you be sure? That doesn't sound like Tom. Whatever would make him change?"

"If I knew the answer to that one I'd know the answer to a lot of things, and probably finding him would be much easier. Tom Marcy changed suddenly, almost overnight. He cleaned up, had his clothes pressed, sent out his laundry, had his shoes shined, and then began doing a lot of running around."

She was obviously puzzled, but whatever she was thinking was suddenly lost by a glance at her watch. She came to her feet suddenly. "I really must go. I've a date with George and that means I must go home and change. If he ever knew I was down here looking like this he would . . ."

Kip got to his feet. "Sure, you can go." Then, before she could protest, he caught her wrist and drew her swiftly to him and kissed her soundly and thoroughly. She pulled away and tried to slap him, but he blocked it with an elbow. "Don't be silly," he said, roughly. "I'm not playing games, but this hotel is a joint.

When you go out of here you're going to look like you should, and your lipstick will be smeared, but good!''

He caught her quickly and kissed her long and thoroughly. She began to struggle again, but he held her and she quieted down. After a moment he let go of her and stepped back. She stared at him, her eyes clouded and her breast heaving. "Did you have to . . . to . . . be so thorough about it?''

"Never do anything by halves," he said. Then he glanced up. "On second thought maybe we should . . .''

"I'm leaving!'' she said hastily, and slipped quickly out the door. He grinned after her, then wiped the back of his hand across his mouth and stared at the red smear, his face sobering. Then he swore softly and dropped into his chair. Despite his efforts he could not concentrate.

He got up and walked to the washbowl and with a dampened towel removed the last of the lipstick.

After all, what did he know? Tom Marcy had been an alcoholic. He had had few friends, and only one or two of those knew him at all well. One was Slim Russell, a wino he occasionally treated, and another had been Happy Day. Marcy had minded his own affairs, and despite his drinking had always been a gentleman.

Something had happened to change Marcy very suddenly. He had straightened up, cleaned up and become very busy—about what?

The pawn ticket might prove something. The ticket was for Tom Marcy's watch. Obviously, he had reached the limit of his funds when some sudden occasion for more money arose, and rather than ask his sister for it, he had hocked his watch.

When he had failed to appear at the restaurant, something that had never happened before, Marilyn had been worried. Several times she had returned to the restaurant, but Tom Marcy had not appeared. Then, as the following month came around, she had returned to the restaurant, and again he had failed to appear. In the meantime she had been watching the papers for any news of death or accident. Then she had hired a detective.

Vin Richards was a shrewd operative with connections throughout the underworld. A week after he had started on the case he was found dead in an alley not far from the hotel in which Kip

Morgan now sat. Vin had taken a knife in the back and a second stab in the ribs. He was very dead when they found him.

Morgan had started fast on the case with a quick check of the morgue, hospitals and accident reports. Then the jails and all of Marcy's old haunts. The result? Nothing, simply nothing at all. Tom Marcy had vanished, dropped into some limbo of forgotten men.

Seven weeks had passed since he had disappeared. Five weeks, or nearly so, before the investigation began. Then Vin Richards, and now—himself.

The pawn ticket answered one question but posed another. Tom Marcy had needed money and hocked his watch, something he apparently had not done before. Why did he need money? If he did need it, why had he not asked Marilyn?

The news clippings now. Two of them were his own idea, and the other two he had found in Marcy's room. But here was a clue, a hint that he was at least on the right track: Two of the clippings, one of his and one of Marcy's, were identical!

It was a news story having to do with the disappearance of one "Happy" Day, a booze hound and clown, long known along East Fifth Street and even as far as Pershing Square. More than one reporter had picked up a good story in the person of Happy, and even the cops who occasionally jailed him liked the man. And then he had dropped from sight. He had been one of Marcy's friends.

Marcy's second clipping was about a fire in a town some sixty miles upstate in which the owner had lost his life. There was little more except that the building had been burned down, a total loss.

The last clipping, one Kip Morgan had obtained himself, was a duplicate of one Tom Marcy had left behind in the hock shop. The operator of the shop, thinking the clipping might be important, had put it away with Tom's watch and had mentioned it to Kip Morgan, then had shown it to him. In a paper of the date of the hocking of the watch, Morgan found the same clipping. It was a simple advertisement for a man to do odd jobs.

The fact that Marcy had it in his fingers when he went to hock his watch seemed to indicate a connection, yet it might not be.

The hocking of the watch might be only an alternative to going to work by answering the ad.

Yet Tom Marcy had straightened up immediately and had begun doing a lot of running around.

Did this advertisement tie up with the disappearance of Happy Day? A sudden hunch had set Morgan checking back through the papers. His hunch had been correct. Such an ad had appeared in the papers just before the disappearance of Happy Day! Now he had a connection, and he had followed it along. Had there been other disappearances? There had.

Slim Russell, Marcy's other friend, had vanished in the intervals between the disappearance of Happy Day and Tom Marcy and from all appearances it had been the vanishing of Slim Russell that had caused the change in Marcy.

Why?

That question offered no solution, but he checked on the approximate date of Russell's disappearance, having only the word of various winos, whose memories were not too good, for that. Yet within a day of Russell's disappearance another such advertisement had been run in the papers!

The newspaper's advertising department was a blind alley. The ad had come by mail and brought the money with it. Cash, no check.

Morgan got up and paced the floor restlessly. Not a breeze stirred and the afternoon was at its hottest, the fan scarcely more than an aggravation. He should be out on a beach now instead of here, sweating out his problem in a cheap hotel. Yet he could not escape the feeling that he was close to something, and moreover, he had the feeling that he was watched.

Richards, cold and cunning as a prairie wolf, a man with many connections and many angles, had been trapped and murdered. Before that, three men had disappeared.

Clearing up the collection, Morgan stowed it away and then, shifting the gun to a spot beneath his coat, which lay at one side of the bed, he sprawled out and fell into a hot, uncomfortable doze.

Vaguely, hours later, his mind fogged by sleep, he felt rather than heard, a faint stirring at the door. His consciousness struggled, then asserted itself. He came out of it and lay very still, every sense alert, listening.

Someone was at the lock! Then, slowly, the knob turned.

CHAPTER TWO

Man in the Pinstriped Suit

Morgan dared not move, for the crack of springs would be audible. The perspiration dried on his face and he strove to keep his breathing even and natural. Now there seemed to be a thicker darkness where the door was open, and then the breeze vanished and he heard the soft click of the door as it closed.

His throat felt tight and his mouth dry. A man with a knife? Gathering himself, he waited, every muscle tense for a sudden lunge.

A floor board creaked faintly, and then a dark figure loomed over the bed. Traffic rumbled in the street outside, and somewhere down the street lights went on and the figure beside the bed was darkly outlined. A hand touched his chest, and Kip saw the other hand lift high, saw the glint of dim light on steel.

With a lunge, he hurled himself up and out, smashing into the body of the intruder. Caught without warning, the man's body crashed back against the wall and the knife clattered to the floor. Yet, instantly, the man lunged upward, seeming to have regained his grasp on the knife, for the glint of it flashed again. Blocking it with a dropped hand to the mans arm, Kip slammed a wicked right into the man's belly. He heard the *whoosh* of breath from lungs, and lifting his fist he smashed at the man's face. The blow landed, but the fellow jerked away and dived for the door.

Kip thrust out a foot and the prowler went sprawling into the hall. But diving after him, Morgan tangled up in a chair and hit the floor himself. He scrambled up, saw a shadow dart into the door of a room across the hall, and sprang after him.

Doors began to open all along the hall and he heard angry complaints. Jerking open the door into the room where the prowler had vanished, Kip saw a man sitting up in bed, swearing and obviously befuddled by sleep. Beyond him, the curtain stirred gently with the breeze from an open window.

162

"What's goin' on?" the man in bed protested sleepily. "Who was that guy?"

"Did you see him?" Morgan stared at the man, but the fellow showed no signs of excitement or heavy breathing, nor did his face show signs of conflict.

"See somebody?" the man almost yelped. "A guy came bustin' through here an' went out that window, runnin' like crazy!"

The alley was dark and the fire escape empty. Whoever the attacker had been, he was safely away by now. Kip Morgan walked back down the hall to his room. They had killed Richards because he was getting too close for comfort, and now they were after him.

When the hotel had quieted down he dressed slowly. It was not late, only a little past ten. He went down the stairs and out into the dingy street. A man slumped against a building nearby, breathing heavily. Another, obviously steeped in alcohol, staggered across the street and lurched against a building, then stared back at Morgan, obviously wondering if the chance of a touch was worth the effort of recrossing the street.

It was still early. Too early for the attacker to have expected Morgan to be in bed unless he *knew* he was there. That implied that the man either lived in the hotel or had a spy on hand, watching him.

Weaving his way down the street through the human driftwood, Morgan considered the problem. The killer of Richards had used a knife, and so had Morgan's attacker. It was imperative that he take every step now with caution, for a killer might await him around every corner. Whatever Tom Marcy had stumbled upon, it led to murder.

Back to the beginning, Marcy had straightened up and quit drinking right after the disappearance of Slim Russell. He had known enough about it to become suspicious, and obviously connected it with the disappearance of Happy Day.

It was not necessarily a coincidence that the two men who had vanished had been known to him, for along these streets the winos nearly all knew each other, at least by sight. Many times they shared bottles or sleeping quarters, and Marcy must have known at least sixty or seventy of them slightly.

Something had made Marcy suspicious, and he had connected the two disappearances. Apparently he had straightened up then and began an investigation on his own. But why? Because of fear? Of some loyalty to these derelicts? Or for some deeper, unguessed reason?

Another question occurred to Morgan. How had the mysterious attacker identified him so quickly? How had he known about Richards? Richards, of course, had been a private dick for several years, but he, Kip Morgan, had never operated in this area nor was he known to the underworld other than by name.

Something had shocked Tom Marcy profoundly, so much that he stopped drinking. An idea was seeping into Morgan's thinking that he was avoiding. To face it meant suspicion of Marilyn Marcy, for how else could the attacker have known of him? Yet why would she hire men, spend good money on their fees and expenses, only to have them killed? If not Marilyn, then someone near her. But neither did that make sense, for the distance from East Fifth to Brantwood was enormous, and those who bridged it were going down, not up. It was a one-way street.

Instead of returning to his hotel, Morgan went to the quiet room Tom Marcy had lived in when not drinking heavily. It was a curious side of the man that during his worst drinking spells he stayed in flop houses or slept out in the hideouts of other winos. In the intervals, he returned to his quiet, cheap little room where he read, slept and seemed to have been happy.

At daybreak Morgan was up and made another close, careful search of the room. It yielded exactly nothing.

Three men missing and one murdered. Two of the men had apparently answered ads. What of Marcy? Had he done the same?

The idea gave Morgan a starting point. He went out into the street. The crowding, pushing, irritable crowd had not yet reached the downtown streets, for the buses and interurbans that fed their streams of humanity into the downtown districts were still gathering their cargoes along the outskirts, miles away.

The warehouse at the address given in the advertisement was closed and still. He walked up the street on the opposite side, then crossed and came back down. Several places were opening for business—a feed store, a filling station on the corner a block away, and a small lunch counter across the way. The warehouse itself was a three-story building, large and old. There was a wooden door, badly in need of paint, a blank, curtained window and on the other side of the door, a large vehicle entrance closed by a metal door sliding down from above.

Kip crossed the street and entered the café. The place was empty but for one bleary-eyed bum down the counter. The waitress, surprisingly, was very neat and attractive. Kip smiled at her, and it was a smile that usually drew a response from women. "How's about a couple of sinkers?" he suggested. "An' a cup of java?"

She brought his order and hesitated beside him. "It's slow this morning."

"Do you have much business here? With all these warehouses I'd think you'd do pretty well."

"Sometimes. A lot of them are working, and our breakfast and lunch business is good. There's just about enough late trade to keep us open. A few cab drivers, newsboys and winos drop in, and some fellows who come around to play the pinball machines."

Kip indicated the warehouse across the street. "Don't they hire a few men once in a while? I saw an ad in the paper a few days ago asking for handymen."

"That place?" She shrugged. "It wouldn't be your sort of work. They hire a few winos and bums, but not many of those. Just a few days each time, I imagine. There was a fellow around here a while back that went to work over there. At least, he hung around for two or three days waiting for someone to show up over there."

"Did he actually get the job?" Morgan's every sense was alert.

"I think so. He waited for them, but when they did open up he just sat around watching for the longest time. He was like all of them, I guess. He just didn't want to work very bad. But he did go over there, I think."

"He hasn't been in since?"

"No. But they haven't been working over there since, either. If they've been around at all, it was at night."

"At night?"

"Yes, I noticed the shade was up part way the other day, and now it's all the way down."

"I'll bet that guy you talked to was the one I knew. We were looking over the papers together," Kip squinted his eyes thoughtfully. "About forty? Medium height, hair turning slightly grey, thin face?"

"That's the one. He was very pleasant, but I think he'd been sick, or else he was just coming off a bad drunk. He was very nice, but kind of jittery. I remember he was wearing a pinstripe suit, very neatly pressed, and you don't see that often down here."

So Marcy had actually been here, watching the warehouse. Kip emptied his cup and pushed it toward her. She filled it, and he put sugar into the coffee and stirred it before speaking again. "What sort of business are they in? Seriously, I'd like to find a job myself. I've got a few bucks, but it won't last forever."

"You've got me. I don't know what they do, although I see a light delivery truck over there sometimes. One of the men comes in here once in a while. He's a blond, stocky, and with a square face. He looks like a Swede I used to know."

Morgan glanced down the counter at the somnolent bum whose head was bowed over his coffee cup.

Through another cup of coffee and a piece of pie, they talked. Twice truck drivers came in and had their coffee and departed, but Kip lingered. They talked of movies, dancing, the latest songs, and a couple of news items, but from time to time they returned to the street and its people. Finally, he had a description of the other man. He was tall, slender and dark of face. He smoked endless cigarettes and drank lots of coffee.

Sometimes they carried bulky boxes or rolls of carpet out of the warehouse, but usually at night.

The bum got slowly to his feet and shuffled to the door. In the doorway he paused and his head turned slowly on his thin neck. For a moment, his eyes met Morgan's. They were clear, sharp and intelligent. Only a fleeting glimpse, and then the head turned again and the man was outside. Kip got slowly to his feet. How much had the man heard? Too much, that was sure. And he was no stew bum, no wino.

*   *   *

Kip walked to the door and stood there, staring up the street at the man who shuffled slowly away. Once, the man paused, then looked back, but Kip was inside the door and out of sight. Obviously, whoever the man was, he had stopped in the door to get a good look at Morgan. He would remember him again.

The man disturbed him, but it could have been only casual interest. Nevertheless, there remained in his mind a haunting sense of familiarity about the man, a sort of half recognition that he could not quite place.

Yet there was no time to waste on that. The next step was obvious. He must find out what went on inside the warehouse, who the two men were, and what was contained in the rolls of carpet or the packing boxes they carried out. These latter had unpleasant connotations to Kip Morgan. More than ever, now, he was sure that Tom Marcy had been murdered.

Except for the narrow rectangle of light where the lunch counter was, all the faces of the buildings were blank and shadowed when Kip Morgan returned. Nor was there movement along the street—only the desolation and complete emptiness that visits such streets long after closing hours. Like another of the derelicts adrift along neighboring streets, Morgan slouched along the street, and at the corner above the warehouse, he turned, walking down a back street until he was opposite the alley that ran beside the warehouse he had been watching.

No one was in sight, and he stepped easily into the shadows of the alley. Then he faded against the wall of the building at the entrance and waited for the space of two minutes. Nobody appeared. Staying in the deeper shadow under the buildings, he went down the alley to the loading space at the rear of the warehouse.

A street light threw a triangle of light into the alley entrance, but the alley itself was in darkness. A rat scurried across the paved loading space, its feet rustling on a sheet of wrapping paper. Kip moved up to the back of the building, then listened. There was no sound from within. He tried the door. It was locked.

There was a platform and a large loading door, but it was immovable. No windows showed on the lower floors, but when he got to the inner corner of the building and glanced up into the darkness of the narrow space between them, he saw a second-story window that seemed to be open. The light was indistinct, but he decided to chance it.

Both walls were brick and without ornamentation, but to a rock climber the task was not great. Moving between the buildings, he put his back to the warehouse and his feet on the opposite wall, and then, in the manner used by rock climbers to climb chimneys, he started up, pushing out on his hands from the wall behind him, and using hands and feet to work his way up. It was a matter of only two or three minutes before he was seated on the sill of the warehouse window.

It was open slightly, propped up by an old putty knife. He listened, and hearing no sound, eased the window higher, then stepped in, returning the window to its former position. Then for several minutes he crouched in the darkness, listening.

Gradually, his ears sorted out the sounds of his nostrils sorted the smells. The creaks and groans normal in an old building, the scurrying of rats. There was the smell of old tar paper, also, and of new lumber. Cautiously, he tried his pencil flash, keeping it away from the windows.

He was in a large, barn-like room that was empty except for some new lumber, a couple of new packing cases, both standing open, and a few tools lying about. Tiptoeing across the floor, he reached the head of the stairs and went down. In the front office there were an old-fashioned safe, a roll-top desk and a couple of chairs. It was dusty and still there, and showed no signs of recent use.

It was in the back office that he made his discovery, and it was little enough, at first, for the lower floor, aside from the front office, seemed unfurnished and empty. And then he saw the partitioned-off room in the corner, and the door standing open.

Inside the room was an old iron cot, a table, washstand and chair. There was a stale, old smell of sweaty clothing and liquor, and the bedding was rumpled and dirty. On the floor were several bottles.

Here, obviously, someone had slept out a drunk, awakening to . . . what? Or had he ever awakened? Or forfeited one sleep for another, the heavy sleep of drunkenness for the silent sleep of death? Morgan shook his head irritably. What reason had he to believe these men were dead? Was he not assuming too much?

He moved around the room. Kicking a rumpled pile of junk in the corner, he disclosed a *blue, pinstriped suit!*

Tom Marcy had worn such a suit when last seen! Dropping to his knees, Kip hastily went through the pockets, but they yielded nothing. He was straightening up when he heard a movement from the alley entrance and a mutter of voices.

CHAPTER THREE

Trapped

Dropping the clothes, he cast one hasty glance around, then darted for the stairway. He went up it on his toes, swiftly and silently, then flattened against the wall, listening.

"Hey? Did you hear something?" The voice was low, gutteral.

"Sure! I heard rats. This old barn is full of them! Come on, let's get that junk and burn it. If the boss ever found out we left anything here he'd cut our hearts out for sure. Where'd you leave it?"

"In the room. I'll get it."

Footsteps plodded across the floor, and then he heard a low exclamation. "Somebody's been here! I never left those clothes like that!"

"Ah, nuts! How can you remember? Who would prowl a dump like this?"

"Somebody's been here! I'm gonna look around."

Kip studied his situation quickly. They would be coming up the steps in a minute, and he hadn't a chance of getting across that wide space of floor and opening the window, then working his way down the wall. Even if his feet did not creak on the boards as he crossed the floor, the act of raising and lowering the window would take too much time, and they would hear his feet scrape on the wall. That thought flashed through his mind, then he wheeled and glanced up. Swiftly and silently he mounted the steps to the unexplored third floor.

He was fairly trapped and he knew it. His hand dropped to the .38 but it was only a reassuring gesture. That would be fatal now. If he ever expected to discover what had become of Marcy, he must avoid bringing the police into the matter, and a shooting would have them around in droves.

Whatever was going on here was shrewdly and efficiently handled, and at the first hint of official interest, would quiet down so fast that no clue would be left. There were few enough as it was.

He could hear the two men stirring around down below. The blond man mumbling to himself, and behind him the protests of the taller, darker man. Twice, Kip got a good look at them in the glow of their own flashlights. Meanwhile, he was working fast. There was a window here, and he eased it up. Down was impossible . . . but up?

Kip glanced out. Opposite the window was the wall, but not a bit over eight feet up was the edge of the roof. Even as he saw his chance, he heard heavy feet on the steps and he scrambled to the sill, balanced an instant after turning his back to the window, then lifted his arms and jumped.

It was a wild, desperate gamble. The only alternative to a shoot-out, which he didn't want. If he fell, a broken leg or neck, and if he was not dead, they soon would have him so. Yet he jumped. His fingers clawed at the parapet edge, then clung. His foot scraped on the wall, and behind him he heard a muttered oath and the clamber of running feet.

Pulling himself up, he swung his feet over the parapet just as the blond man lunged to the window. For a startled instant, their eyes met, and then he was up and running across the roof. Ducking behind a chimney, he heard the sharp bark of a pistol shot, and brick fragments spattered behind him. With the chimneys between them, he reached the far side of the roof and threw himself over the parapet, held for an instant, then dropped.

But he did not dart across the roof for shelter of more chimneys, for here there was a space between the buildings, and he decided to chance it. He braced his back against one side, his feet against the other, and started down, moving swiftly as possible. When the running feet reached the edge of the roof, he stopped, holding himself still.

"Where'd he go?" The dark man was genuinely excited now.

"Across the roofs! Where else? Let him go, or we'll have the cops on us!"

"Yeah, let's beat it!"

They vanished, and he worked his way swiftly down the rest of the way and hastily brushed himself off. He walked to the alley entrance, hearing the scream of a siren. Then he stepped out into the street and walked toward his car, almost a block away.

He had just seated himself in the car when he saw a light grey coupé whisk by. The man nearest him was the blond man.

Kip started his car, letting the grey coupé get a start, then pulled into the street and followed. Habitually, he went bareheaded, but he kept a supply of hats and caps in the car to be used on just such tailing jobs, and now he pulled on a wide-brimmed grey hat, and pulled down the brim.

The grey coupé swung onto Wilshire and started out along the boulevard. It was late and there was little traffic, so after holding to his position on the tail of the coupé as long as he dared, Morgan let his car come abreast and pass the coupé. He made a left turn two blocks ahead and swung around the block.

When he emerged to pick up the trail again his lights were on dim and he wore a battered, narrow-brimmed hat. Moreover, his car now had a double taillight showing.

Shortly after reaching Beverly Hills the coupé swung right and Kip pulled in to the curb, switched hats again and turned on his lights to full brightness. Just as the other car pulled up to the curb and stopped, he wheeled by, going fast. He did a right turn and parked, then slid from the seat, hatless now and walked back to the corner.

The two men had started diagonally across the street toward a large house set back a little from the street, the lawn surrounded by trees and a hedge. As the two men stepped into the shadow of the hedge, a car pulled up and stopped. A man and a woman got out, and as they started across the walk, the blond man stepped from the shadows.

"Mr. Villani? I got to see you."

The man was tall and heavily built. He wore evening clothes, and as Morgan closed in, he could hear the irritation in the man's

voice as he replied. "All right, Gus. Just a minute." He turned
to the girl. "Would you mind going on in, Marilyn? I'll follow in
a minute."

The girl's face turned into the light, and Kip jumped as if
touched, with an electric wire. *It was Marilyn Marcy!*

He drew deeper into the shadows of the hedge, scowling. It
didn't make sense, none of it. Then his attention was drawn to
the two men who had drawn nearer the man called Villani. The
latter was angry. "Gus, how many times have I told you not to
come near me? You know how to reach me, and that's the only
way! Get me?"

Gus' voice was low in protest. There was anxiety in it, too,
and some fear. "But, Boss!" He protested. "This is bad now!
That dick, Morgan, has been to the warehouse, I think!"

"Inside?" Villani demanded.

"Uh-huh. I don't know if it was him, but I think so."

"I think it was, Boss," the taller man said, "but he got away
and we only had a glimpse of him."

Morgan waited, trying to see Villani's face better. This man
was the boss, the man he wanted to trace. And he knew Marilyn
Marcy.

A low-voiced colloquy followed, but what was said Morgan
did not know, and try as he might he could hear no more than a
few words, and then a low mumble of sound. "All right, Vinson.
Stay with him. We can have no failure this time!" Those parting
words he heard, and he saw the two men turn away and walk
toward their car. He wondered about following them, finally
decided nothing could be gained. Rather, he wanted to know
what was going on here.

Instead, as Villani disappeared within the house and the grey
coupé drove off, he walked down the street, turned and walked
two blocks to a corner drugstore. A swift check after the name of
Villani in the phone directory brought him to the correct address.
The name was *George* Villani!

Marily had had a date with George. That tied in, but what did
it mean? If she was double-crossing Morgan, what did she figure
to gain by it? On the other hand, suppose she didn't know? And
suppose that was how the crooks had found out about Morgan

and about Vin Richards? Because she had simply told her boy friend.

Morgan turned the corner and walked up to the car, then stopped, his stomach suddenly hollow and his mouth dry. The thin, dark man was standing beside a tree near the car, and he had a gun in his hand. "Hello, Morgan," he said. "It looks like we're going to get together after all! Nice rig you've got here, all the hats and everything. You had me fooled."

"Then what made you stop here?" Kip asked pleasantly.

"The car. It looked familiar, and it was like the one we saw when we left the warehouse. For luck, we had a look. You shouldn't leave your registration card on the steering post."

"Well, so here we are." Morgan couldn't see the blond man and that worried him. He had an idea that Gus was the tough one. This guy thought he was tough, but Gus was the man who worried Kip. "You'd better put that rod away. Somebody will see you."

"There's nobody around." The dark man, Vinson, liked this. He had been seeing a lot of movies and he was acting the casual tough guy. "You've been getting in my hair, Morgan. We don't like guys who get in our hair."

Kip shrugged, and the gun tilted a little. This guy was hair-triggered, and maybe that was as good as it might be bad. "It's my business. Where's Tom Marcy?"

"Marcy?" That obviously surprised Vinson. "I never heard of any guy named Marcy. What's the angle?"

'Why, I'm looking for him. That's my job." Morgan was alert and curious, for obviously Vinson was puzzled and surprised.

Vinson stared at him. "I don't get it, chum. We figured you for an . . ." he stopped, catching himself on the word. "We figured you for a dick."

"Look," Morgan said, "something's screwy about this. I'm looking for a guy named Marcy. If you don't know him, then we've got no business together. Let's forget it. You go your way and I'll go mine, and everybody'll be happy."

"Are you nuts?" Vinson stared at him. "We're taking you where we can ask some questions—an' we'll get answers." His eyes flickered. "Here comes the—"

Morgan lunged, swinging down and across with his left hand.

It slapped the gun aside, and his right swept up to grab the barrel, missed, but he followed through the miss by driving the butt of his palm under Vinson's chin. The gangster's heels flew up and he hit the sidewalk, the gun flying from his hand.

Kip heard a grunt behind him and the sound of running feet, and he threw himself into the hedge, felt branches tear at him, and then he was through and sprinting across the lawn. He ducked quickly behind a tree, grabbed a low branch and heaved himself up. Almost at once both men were rushing toward him.

Motionless in the tree, he waited, every sense alert. Yet they rushed by beneath him, then paused. "You fool!" Gus snarled. "You should have shot him!"

He heard them searching through the brush, but the branches over their heads never seemed to occur to them as a hiding place. A light went on in the house, and with a mutter of voices, the two men slipped out of the yard. Several minutes later he heard their car start.

Kip Morgan eased back against the trunk of the tree and sat still, taking his time before moving. There was always the chance it had been another car, or that they had driven off but a short distance to watch for him. He was in no hurry now, either. He had plenty to think about.

George Villani was apparently the boss. Whatever was going on, he was the man who gave the orders, for when serious trouble came up, they had come at once to him. And George Villani was dating Marilyn Marcy. The answer to that was problematical, but it seemed apparent that through him the killers had learned of Vin Richards, and Marilyn must have told him that Morgan was holed up in the hotel.

Carefully Kip lowered himself from the tree. He did not go into the street from which he had come but worked his way along the hedge toward the rear of the property, and finding a gate there, went through into the alley.

His car could wait until daylight. If they watched it and he returned now they would kill him without hesitation. Yet once in the alley, Kip halted, scowling.

Marilyn was still next door, and he could hear sounds of music and laughter from the house. Evidently a small party was in process. He hesitated, half of a mind to crash the party, but his shirt was rumpled and his clothes dusty from crawling around the old buildings. He crossed several streets, then caught a cab and returned to his own apartment. For this night the room at the hotel could stay empty.

As he considered the situation he became convinced that Tom Marcy must have come upon some hint of a danger that threatened his sister. Perhaps in some way he had established a connection between Villani and the disappearances of Day and Russell. It would account for his sudden change, his ceasing to drink and his investigations. The danger of his sister marrying a murderer had started him digging into the strange warehouse on the street of missing men.

Back in his apartment he pulled off his shoes and sat half dressed on the edge of the bed. Tomorrow would be soon enough, but tomorrow he would have to bear down. He must know why those men had vanished, and what had been done with Tom Marcy.

He slept, and he dreamed, a dream of flames, of a scream in the night, of . . . He awoke suddenly and saw Vinson leaning over him, saw Gus standing at the door, a gun in his hands. He started to sit up, and Vinson swung a riding boot he had picked up. The heel struck Kip on the temple. Something exploded in his brain and he lunged, blind with pain, to get off the bed. His feet tangled in the bed clothes and he lit sprawling. Then the boot crashed down on the back of his head, and he hit the floor on his face.

When he regained consiousness he was lying in the darkness of a delivery truck and the first thing his opened eyes detected was the glisten of light on a shoe toe, polished and bright. That toe was only inches from his face. Closing his eyes to slits, he lay still, pain throbbing in his skull, and fought to make some sense of his situation.

Somehow they had traced him and gained access to his room without awakening him. Knocked out, he had been loaded in the truck and was now being taken . . . where?

Listening, he decided by the lack of traffic sounds and the unbroken rate of speed that they were somewhere out on the highway, far from Los Angeles.

"What did he say to do with him?" That was Vinson's voice.

"Hold him. The boss wants to talk to him." That was Gus, then, sitting over him. "He wants to know did he talk to somebody."

Tentatively, Kip tried his muscles. He could not move his hands, for they were bound tightly. He relaxed, letting the hammers in his skull pound away with their monotonous throbbing.

Suddenly the car made an abrupt turn and the road became rough. A gravel road and badly corrugated. The car dipped down several times, then climbed and continued to climb in slow spirals, higher and ever higher. The air was clear and cool, and then the truck made another sharp turn and after several minutes came to a halt. Morgan let his muscles relax completely.

"Haul him out," Vinson said. "I'll light up."

Gus opened the doors from within and dropped out to the ground, then he grabbed Morgan's ankles and jerked, then jerked again. Morgan hit the road with a thump. It was all he could do to keep from crying out as his head thumped the tailboard, then the ground. Gus grabbed him by the front of his shirt and dragged him to the door of a dugout and, opening it, threw him into the darkness. Kip heard the door slam shut and the hasp drop in place, and then he was alone in utter darkness.

CHAPTER FOUR

Into the Pit

For what seemed a long time he lay still, the throbbing in his head absorbing all his attention until the pain was a great sea that seemed to send wave after wave over him. His head felt enormous and the slightest move stirred him to new agonies. Yet through it, fear began clawing a way, tearing at the pain that drowned his consciousness, hammering for attention at the portals of his thinking processes. They would come back, Vinson and Gus. The only way to escape more pain and even death was to endure the pain now, to fight now, while he had a moment's freedom from their watching eyes.

He lunged, bucking with his bound body, then rolling until he had turned over three times and found himself against a tier of boxes or crates. Boxes, from the solid feel of them. Hunching himself into a sitting position, he began sawing the ropes at his wrists against the sharp corner of the box. In his desperation he jerked too far and the edge scraped his wrist. Wildly, his pain driving reason from his mind, he fought to cut loose the ropes, but they were good ropes and had been drawn tight.

Still he struggled on. The close confines of the dugout made him pant, and sweat soaked his shirt and ran into his eyes, smarting and stinging. His muscles grew heavy with weariness, but he would not stop, but fought with all his strength, and to no avail. The ropes seemed to have chafed, but no more. So intent was he on his struggles that he failed to hear the footsteps approaching, failed to hear the door open. Only when the powerful flashlight blinked in his eyes did he look up, startled and afraid.

"Finally woke, huh?" Gus strode over to him and jerked him away from the boxes, glancing at the ropes. "Trying to escape huh?" Gus drew back his toe and booted him in the ribs.

With a knife he slashed the ropes that bound Kip's ankles, then jerked him to his feet. Morgan's feet felt heavy, as though he wore diving shoes. Gus put a hand between his shoulder blades and shoved him at the door, and Morgan reached it in a stumbling run. The light of the flash shot past him, illuminating the edge of a wash not fifty feet away.

A wash . . . or a canyon. Ten feet or two hundred. His stumbling run changed to a real run and he hurled himself, bending far forward as he ran, toward that edge and whatever it might offer him.

There was a startled curse, then a yell, a momentary pause, another yell of warning, and then a bullet slammed past his ear and a gun barked. Kip left his feet and dived for the edge. Head first he plunged, in a rattle of gravel and loose stones, over the brink.

He fell, then brought up with a crunch and a mouthful of sand at the bottom of the wash. Lunging to his feet, wrists still bound behind him, he charged blindly into the night down the wash. His feet were prickling with a million tiny needles at every step, but he ran, wildly, desperately, raw breath cutting at his lungs.

Then, suddenly aware that his running made too much sound, he slid to a stop and listened. There were running footsteps somewhere, and a shaft of light shot across the small plateau of a mine dump as the cabin door opened. He heard angry shouts, swearing, and then the car started.

Kip Morgan had no idea where he was. His brain was pounding painfully, and he smarted from a dozen scratches and bruises. Yet he walked on, holding to the wash and fighting at his bonds with utter futility. The black maw of another wash opened on his right and he turned into that, found a steep path, and painstakingly made his way up it, crouching to keep low as he crossed the skyline of the wash.

How far he walked he had no idea, but he pushed on along the mountain, wanting only distance between himself and the searchers. As the first faint intimations of dawn began to lighten the eastern sky, he dropped to a sitting position beside a boulder, and, his hands still bound, was almost instantly asleep.

The hot morning sun awakened him, and he got up, conscious of a dull throbbing in his hands. Twisting to get a look at them, he found them badly swollen and slightly blue. Worried and frightened by the look of them, he got to his feet and stared around. He was, judging by the sun, on the eastern slope of a mountain. All around was desert, with no indication of life anywhere. Not a sound disturbed the vast stillness of the morning, and there was no movement.

Turning, he started along a shoulder of the mountains, feeling positive that he was likely to find some sign of life on the western side. He must have been brought over the mountains from the coast during the night.

His mouth was dry, and he realized the intense heat, even though it could be no more than nine or ten oclock, was already having its effect. Stumbling over the rocks, he hurried on, and suddenly, ahead of him, he saw a road.

It was the merest trail, with no tracks upon it, but it had to go somewhere, so he followed it. When he had gone no more than a mile, he rounded a turn in the road and found himself facing the ramshackle hoist house and gallows frame of an abandoned mine. He stumbled toward it. An ancient door sagged on its hinges, the rusty cable that led to the shiv wheel hung loose, and as he neared the buildings a pack rat scurried out of the way.

Several tracks of small animals led toward the wall of the mountain beyond the small ledge on which the mine stood, and he followed them, finding a trickle of water running from a pipe thrust into the rock. When he had finished drinking he turned and staggered toward the hoist house, searching for something with which he might cut his bonds. On the floor was the rusty blade of a round-point shovel.

Dropping to his knees, he backed his feet toward the shovel and got it on edge between them. Then, holding it with his feet, he began to saw steadily, rubbing the ropes that bound his wrists against the edge of the shovel.

Every moment was excruciating, but stubbornly he refused to rest even for a minute, chafing stoically at the ropes, able to make only short strokes, but bearing down as much as he could. Finally he felt a rope give, and after a few minutes of struggling his hands were free. He brought them around before him and stared at them.

They were grotesquely swollen, puffed like a child's boxing gloves, with a tight band of identification around his wrists where the ropes had been. Returning to the spring he dropped on his knees and thrust his hands under the cold trickle of water.

For a long time he knelt there, uncertain as to how much good it was doing but enjoying the feet of the cold water on his hands. Finally he gave it up. Time would do more good now than anything, and there was much to do. Taking a long drink, he turned away from the mine, but before leaving he glanced around for a weapon and found a short piece of rusty drill steel a foot and a half long. Hefting it, he liked the feel, even with his puffed hands, so he thrust it into his belt and headed west.

As he walked he carried his hands shoulder high for they ached less, and after a few miles they even felt better. Suddenly, through a break in some trees ahead, he saw the pavement of a highway, and the first truck along stopped to pick him up. He rode to town in it.

Once again back in Marcy's room, he ran the bowl full of hot water. He soaked his hands, and after a while they began to feel better. As he soaked them, he considered the situation.

So far he had done little, although he seemed to have Villani and his two men badly upset. No doubt they believed him to know more than he actually did. He was positive they had murdered Tom Marcy, but he had no evidence of any description, nor could he even suggest a motive. As things stood, he could go to the law and he might swear out a warrant for their arrest for assault, kidnapping, and possibly a few other things. Proving it against good lawyers, and George Villani would have the best, would be something else.

What did he have? Three men had disappeared, at least two of them after answering ads that had taken them to the warehouse. Vin Richards had been murdered.

He dug out the clippings again and studied them, and again he was faced with the clipping concerning the fire. That alone failed to fit. Suddenly, it hit him right between the eyes. What if the body in the fire had not been that of the owner? *What if the owner was involved in a plot with Villani to rook the insurance companies? With Villani supplying the bodies?*

Hastily he dried his hands and grabbed up the phone, dialing the number of the newspaper that published the item. In a matter of minutes he had the name of the insurance company concerned. The city editor asked, "What's the rumble? Anything wrong up there?"

Morgan hesitated. Then, remembering the breaks the papers had given him in his fighting days, and how shrewd some of their men had been, he said carefully, "I'm not sure. Something smells to high heaven, but maybe I'm a screwball. Three men disappeared off skid row in the last few months and somebody seems mighty anxious not to have it investigated."

"Who is this talking?"

"Kip Morgan. I used to be a fighter."

"I remember. But you were the guy who busted that marijuana racket, weren't you? How about me sending a man over to talk to you and get the story?"

"Uh-uh." Kip hesitated. "Have him get all he can on George Villani and two guys named Gus and Vinson, and the address at 422 Cooper."

As he hung up, he reflected with satisfaction that now the papers had a suggestion and they would follow it up. Also if anything happened to him they would be curious. It took him just fifteen minutes by cab to get to the office of the insurance company and the man he wanted to see. He had heard a good deal of Neal Stoska, the insurance company's investigator.

Stoska was a thin, angular man with shrewd, thoughtful eyes. He leaned back in his swivel chair. "What is it you wish to know?" he asked cautiously.

"Your company insured a building up in Margaux that had a bad fire a short time ago. Is that right?"

"No," Stoska replied. "We insured Leonard Buff, the man who was burned. Tri State insured the building. Why do you ask?"

"Just curious. I was wondering if it looked all right to you? I mean, was there anything phony connected with it?"

Stoska's face seemed to sharpen and his eyes grew intent. "Why do you ask?" he said quietly, then suddenly turned impatient. "Morgan, you must know we can't discuss such matters with just anybody who walks into this office. If I did suspect that anything was wrong we would certainly be in no position to talk about the matter. If we could make a case, naturally, we'd go to court. Have you any information for us?"

"Listen . . ." Kip Morgan sat back in his chair and quietly told his story from the beginning. The Marcy case, his check on the disappearance of Day and of Slim Russell, and all that had occured since. "It's a wild yarn," he finished, "but true, and I could use some help."

"You think Marcy was the body in that fire?"

"No, I think that was Russell's body. I think Marcy discovered something accidentally. He probably went with Russell and waited in the café while Slim applied for the job. Slim never came back, and it's possible that Marcy saw Villani near that building, or with one of the men from the building. One thing or another made him suspicious, and he was a man who loved his sister. In fact, his love for her was the only real thing in his life."

"It's all guesswork," Stoska agreed, "but good guesswork. You had something you wanted me to check?"

"Yes. The size of the dead man and the size of Russell. Slim was a war veteran, so you can get his size that way, or from the police. They probably picked him up and mugged him several times."

Stoska reached for the phone and at the same time pressed a button for a file clerk. "Get me the file on Buff," he said, "all there is on him. Also," he added, "put through a call to Tri State and ask Gordon to come over. Tell him it's important."

A voice sounded on the phone. Morgan grinned, for from the sharp, nasal sound it was Mooney. In reply to Stoska's question, Mooney read off, after a brief interval, a description of Slim Russell. As he read, Stoska glanced over at Morgan and nodded. When he hung up, he turned back to Kip. "It fits," he said gravely. "I remember what we had on Buff. They were the same size."

Kip's cab dropped him at Marilyn Marcy's apartment and he went up fast. She was alone, but dressed to go out.

"What is it?" She crossed the room to him quickly. "You've found him? He's—he's dead? Gone?"

"Take it easy." He dropped into a chair. "Fix me a drink, will you?" he asked. She was frightened, he could see, and felt that the activity might relieve the situation a bit. "No," he added, "I haven't found him, but you've talked too much."

"I've talked!" She turned to him, her eyes wide. "Why, I've done no such thing! I've—"

"Shut up!" he said impatiently. "Finish that drink and come over here. You talked, and you got Vin Richards killed, and you came near to getting me killed. A guy jumped me with a shiv not more than a couple of hours after you left my hotel room! That was your doing, honey."

"I don't believe it!" she flared. "Anyway, I told no one!"

"What about George?" he demanded.

"Well," she said defensively, "what about him? Of course, I told him. I've told him everything. I'm engaged to him."

"You won't be long," he said grimly. "Now sit down and get this straight the first time. I haven't a lot of time to waste and I don't want to go into any involved explanations. When I get through you're probably going to call me a liar, but that's neither here nor there. You hired me to do a job."

"And I don't like the way you talk!" she flared. "I think I've had about enough of your coming up here and ordering me around! You're fired!"

"All right," he said, "so I'm fired. I'm still on this case because it's become mighty damned personal since I last talked to you. Guys don't put the arm on me and get away with it. Now listen: You talked, all right. You talked to George Villani, and you'd better know that if your brother is dead, Villani killed him, or had him killed!"

She came off the chair and to her full height, her face drained of color, her eyes bright. "Of all the preposterous cock-and-bull stories—"

He reached out and put his hand on her shoulder and pushed gently. She sat down abruptly. "Sit still," he said. "You told George Villani about hiring Richards. Within a few days, Richards is dead. You told Villani about me, and where I was, and within a few hours, a guy jumps me with a knife. Who else knew? Who else could have known?"

She stared at him, her face white. Slowly, she blinked. She tasted her drink. Then she shook her head. "It doesn't add up. What would he gain? George didn't even know about Tom, as I'd never told him. And why should he kill him?"

"Tom loved you." Morgan watched her over the glass, and he could see that she was thinking now. Her anger and astonishment had faded. "What if he saw you with a guy he knew was a wrong gee? Don't ask me how he knew, but Tom Marcy had been around, and he was always skating along the edge of the underworld. He knew a lot of people.

"I don't believe," he continued, "that Villani knew Tom Marcy was your brother. He only knew him as a guy who was doing some interfering. Or that's how it was at first. When you told him about Richards, about your brother missing, then he may have put two and two together."

Briefly and quietly, he explained, but saying nothing about the papers he had talked to, or about the insurance company. "What does Villani do?" he asked finally.

"Do?" She shrugged. "He's a contractor of some kind, does some building. I never talked business with him very much, but he always has plenty of money, and is apparently successful."

"Well," Kip said, gulping his liquor, "don't ask him any questions now. Leave him to me."

The buzzer sounded suddenly, and she came to her feet, her eyes wide. "That's George! He was calling for me, and I'd forgotten!"

"Don't let this bother you," Kip advised, "and don't ask any questions. If he got suspicious now he might start on you next. When a man begins to kill as callously as this man has, then he never knows when to stop. Be careful!"

There was a light tap on the door, and Marilyn crossed to it, opening to admit George Vallani.

CHAPTER FIVE

No Bargains in Blood

He was a big man, broad shouldered and deep in the chest. His eyes went quickly to Kip Morgan and they darkened perceptibly. "George," Marilyn said, smiling. "I want you to meet Kip Morgan. He's the detective I've got looking for Tom."

"How do you do?" Villani said affably. "Having any luck?"

"Sure," Kip said, unable to resist needling the big man. "We'll break the whole case in a matter of hours."

Villani smiled, but there was no humor in it. "Isn't that what detectives always say?"

Morgan shrugged, but some devil within made him push the matter further. Suddenly all his resentment at this man began to well to the surface. He knew it was foolish, yet he could not resist deliberately baiting him. "Maybe. I don't know what detectives always say. I know this one is a cinch! The guy," he added, enjoying Marilyn's tenseness, "has been a dope all along. He's been mixed up in a dirty racket, we think, supplying bodies to folks who want to collect insurance, and getting his bodies off skid row where the drifters and no-goods are, the men nobody is supposed to be interested in."

"Seems far-fetched," Villani said, no suggestion of a smile on his face now. "Wouldn't the insurance companies be suspicious?"

Kip grinned. Suddenly, he felt good. He never had been much of a hand at beating around the bush or ferreting out clues. He was a direct-action man, and he liked to bull right into the middle of things and keep crowding a crook until he acted without thinking. Careful planning is foolproof in many cases until the planner is pushed so fast he can't plan and has to ad lib his movements and his talking.

"Sure," he said, "the insurance companies are suspicious. I made them suspicious. So are the papers. Now all we've got to do is pick up the boys this guy has working for him and make them talk. Once they let their hair down we'll have the big guy, but fast!"

Vallini didn't like that. He didn't like it a bit. Kip Morgan was curious, and he knew what the next action should be. Villani had no reason to believe he was suspected, but all the reason in the world now to want to cover up fast. And the next move for Vallani was to rid himself of the two who might talk. That done, the chances were that he would be in the clear.

Villani seemed to have come to the same conclusion. He turned to Marilyn. "I'd no idea you were busy," he said. "Why don't we skip our dinner date tonight? I've a few things I should attend to, and no doubt you want to finish your conference with Mr. Morgan."

"Why . . ." Marilyn started, but Kip interrupted.

"That would help, all right. There are several things we haven't taken up yet, and they should be discussed."

"Fine!" Villani was obviously relieved. "I'll call you, dear." He turned to Morgan. "And you have my best wishes. I hope you find your men!"

As the door closed, Marilyn turned to Kip, her face stiff. "He couldn't get away too fast, could he? What is the trouble?"

"Trouble?" Morgan was thinking fast. "Why, none. Not for us, at least. As for Gus and Vinson—I wouldn't want to be in their shoes. He's going to kill them. He's headed for them now!"

He finished his drink and grinned at her, real regret in his eyes. "I'd like to spend the evening with you, but I've got to follow him."

She caught up her coat and hat. "Then what are we waiting for? Let's go!"

"Not you!" he protested. "You can't go!"

"I'm going." She turned her eyes on him. "Tom Marcy was my brother."

He hesitated no longer. "It's your funeral, but remember I told you this was no place for a woman. No telling where we'll be before this night is over!"

Villani was getting into his car as they reached the street, and Marilyn tugged at Kip's arm. "Come on! My car's right across the alley!"

As they swung into the street, Villani was rounding the corner headed for the boulevard, and he was traveling fast. Yet he followed the boulevard only a short distance, turning off and heading for his own place. They watched him turn in against the curb as they drifted past, lights out. Then Morgan touched her arm. "Right down the street here is my car. We'd better take it. He won't recognize it as he will yours."

They switched cars and sat in the darkness, waiting. Both of them were tense. Kip Morgan knew that before this night was gone there would be serious trouble, for Villani was not a man to be taken easily, nor was Gus. Vinson—well, he might fight like a cornered rat. The girl beside him disturbed him more than he would have guessed. And it was not only that he feared for her, it was something much more than that. She did things to him, and that wasn't good. Not tonight.

Villani came from his house on the run and sprang into his car. He did a fast U-turn in the middle of the street and the headlights sprayed across their car. Kip, seeing what was to come, had ducked down and pressed Marilyn Marcy down with him. Her face was invitingly near, and he kissed her, simply, quickly, but effectively.

When the lights were gone he straightened up and let the clutch out. They started rolling and turned the corner on two wheels to catch the turn of the big convertible ahead of them. Wherever Villani was going he wasn't in a hurry.

After a half-mile, Kip switched his lights to dim and gained speed, changing hats, also. Villani glanced back once, but apparently had no idea he was followed. He headed over the pass toward San Fernando, and Kip tailed him.

At a filling station near a motel, Morgan swung suddenly to the roadside. "Get to a phone," he said swiftly, "call Stoska at this number and tell him what's happened." Kip grabbed a map from the seat beside him and with his pen, drew a swift circle. "Tell him we're headed for an abandoned mine in that vicinity and to get hold of the sheriff and get out there, and fast!"

Marilyn slid from the car and even as she took her first step away from it, Kip was opening up and traveling fast, headed after Villani. He overtook him as he was swinging off into the hills and followed, his lights on bright again now. After a short distance he swung the car into a side road, switched off his lights and backed out. From then on he followed without lights.

For some reason Gus and Vinson must still be at the mine, Kip decided, or else Villani was expecting them there soon. When he saw the lights turn in at the mine road, Kip followed on only a little further, then stopped his car and climbed out. From a hidden panel under the dash he took a Colt .45 automatic and followed on up the hill. His car was hidden in the brush, invisible from the road at night, and to get out, Villani would have to come this way.

All was still at the mine. The car stood in the open space near the gallows frame, but the delivery truck was nowhere to be seen. There was a light in the shack.

Kip Morgan moved to the hoist house and inside in the dark he crouched and waited. Without doubt Gus and Vinson would soon be here. Villani had made his rendezvous with them at a place where their bodies would not be found. He would shoot first and fast, then drop the bodies down the shaft and get away. The scheme had every chance of succeeding.

What little he knew would not tie Villani to the crimes. There might be more evidence, but with Gus and Vinson unable to talk, proving a case might be very difficult.

He had been hearing the car for several minutes before it swung into the yard. It was the truck.

Vinson and Gus got out. They whispered together for a minute, then went to the shack and walked in. Kip moved from the hoist house and, circling, keeping to the deeper shadow near the buildings, got to the wall of the shack. As he stepped close to the wall beside a window, he heard the front door open and close. He held himself, listening, but heard no footsteps. Voices sounded and he pressed his ear against the wall.

Vinson was sitting at the table, and Villani was pacing the floor. "What were you doing?" Villani's voice was icy. "Sleeping on the job? The man was tied so tight he was absolutely helpless! How could he get away?"

"I sure don't know," Vinson said sullenly. "Don't blame me! He's a hard guy to hold."

Villani was pacing nearer and nearer to the shelf behind Vinson. On that shelf lay a piece of drill steel, not unlike that Kip himself had taken from the mine the day before. Vinson stared at his hands as they rested on the table. "Anyway," he was pleading, "Gus was there, too!"

Villani stopped pacing and his hand reached for the drill steel and took a firm grip. He lifted it clear of the shelf and . . . Suddenly gravel crunched at the corner of the house and Kip Morgan wheeled. A gun flamed not a dozen feet away, and he felt the bullet tug at his clothes. Only his sudden movement had saved him. Instantly, he fired. Gus caught himself in midstride and fired again. That bullet thudded into the wall, and as Kip fired a second and third time, the man went down, rolling over on the gravel.

Drawing back, Kip flattened against the wall and glanced in. Instantly, he turned his face away, sick to the stomach. There was no sign of Villani inside the shack, but the door was open a crack. Vinson was surely dead, for no man could be alive with his skull smashed like that.

Kip glanced around. Probably Villani had only sent Gus out to be rid of him while he killed Vinson, planning to get Gus later. The shots outside had warned him that Gus had actually found something, somebody. Now he knew he had one man to kill, and possibly two. The slightest move might bring a shot. Kip moved in spite of that, going toward the front of the house, reasoning that Villani would move around the other side to the rear, as Gus had done. At the front of the house, he took three careful steps to the truck and slid behind it.

A slow minute dribbled away and then another. He waited, every sense alert, but there was no nearby sound. Faintly, somewhere off in the mountains, he heard a car. The sound seemed miles away in the calm, clear air.

"Morgan!" It was Villani calling. "Is that you out there? Let's talk business!"

Kip lay very still, waiting him out. For a few seconds no sound came, and then Villani said persuasively, "Morgan, this is foolish. What Marilyn can pay you doesn't warrant risking your life. I've done very well, and I've got money. Above all, I've got some of it here with me. A thousand dollars if you'll call it quits!"

Morgan said nothing. He had eased himself down on the gravel now and he could see dimly the area from which the voice came. Only Gus' body was visible.

"A thousand dollars is a lot of money," Villani continued, "and much more than you'll get from Marilyn. You've not found Marcy, I know that, so all you can get is what she's paying you by the day. I offer a thousand dollars. You say the word, I'll toss it to you, and you can slip away as you like."

Kip rested his gun barrel across his forearm. "And have you shoot me while I'm in the open? Nothing doing!"

Deliberately, he was prolonging the discussion to try and locate Villani. He might only get one shot, and it had to be good.

"I'll wrap a stone around it and toss it right to you," Villani protested. "You're in no danger!"

"A thousand isn't enough," Kip said, conversationally. "I may not get much from Marilyn Marcy, but that insurance company will pay off like a slot machine."

There was a brief silence. "All right, two thousand, and you'll not get that from any insurance company!"

"Make it five thousand," Morgan replied. "I like the sound of it better."

Villani was growing desperate as the minutes slid by and he was held still. He wanted to leave, to get clear out of California, and fast.

"All right." Kip's gun was ready. "Wrap it around a stone and toss it to me. Tie your handkerchief around it all."

Suddenly they both heard the crunch of feet on the trail, and Kip stiffened. He started to yell a warning, and then she had come on, Marilyn Marcy, walking fast and unaware of the situation into which she was coming. *"Marilyn!"* Kip yelled. *"Get back! Get back fast!"*

"No you don't!" Triumph was hoarse in Villani's throat. "Stay right where you are or I'll kill you!"

The situation had changed and Villani was completely in control, unless . . .

With a lunge, Kip dived around the car and rushed for the building. A gun roared, and then he fired and knew he had missed, but he saw the dark figure of Villani lunge up from the ground, heard both their guns roar again, and then he swung his barrel down in a chopping blow. But Villani swerved, the blow took Kip off balance, and Villani's own blow knocked the gun from his hand when the gun barrels met in mid-air.

Morgan threw his right then, low and hard. His fist, still swollen from the tight lashings of the previous night numbed with pain as the blow landed, but he charged, hurling his weight against the bigger man and grabbing his gun wrist with his left. He chopped again at the body with his right, found the blow blocked, and then whipped over a short hook to the neck, purposely keeping the punch low to avoid injuring his fist.

It landed, and Villani staggered. Instantly Kip whipped his elbow high and hard across the man's face, then jerked back with it, and slammed Villani back against the building. The gun roared and the bullet kicked gravel over Kip's shoes, and then the gun left Villani's hands and Kip jerked the butt of his palm hard against the killer's chin.

Villani's head slammed back and Kip caught a raking punch to the face, and then hooked low and hard with both hands. Villani gasped and dropped.

Gasping for breath, Kip Morgan stepped around the fallen man and retrieved both guns. He could hear other cars on the trail as Marilyn ran to him, avoiding Villani. "Are you hurt? Are you all right?"

"I'm all right," he said. "Did you get word to them?"

"They're coming now, I think," she replied. "They told me to wait, but I hurried. I thought I might help. Was I wrong?"

He looked at her, exasperated, then shrugged, smiling. "No, everything turned out all right."

Villani started to get up.

"Stay where you are," Kip told him. "Lie down flat. There, that's better."

"That offer goes," Villani said, the words fumbling past his swollen lips. "I've got twenty thousand here. I'll give you half to let me go."

"Nothing doing. What became of Tom Marcy?"

"Suppose you find out?" Villani sneered. "You've nothing on me!"

Two cars were pulling into the yard. "No?" Kip smiled. "I've murder against you. The murder of Vinson, killed in the shack. Your prints will be on that drill steel you used to kill him."

Stoska, Mooney and a dozen other men piled out, and Villani was jerked to his feet. During the hurried explanations, Marilyn stood close beside Kip.

He was feeling it now, and was sore in every muscle as well as physically exhausted. The struggle to escape, his hands from which most of the swelling had gone but which were still sore, the fight and all the tension of the past days was piling up.

Stoska listened, nodding from time to time. "We checked that body again," he said, "and there are some discrepancies, but very slight. However, we're going into a very thorough study of several other fires recently in which bodies have been found."

Mooney turned his head and looked at Marilyn. "We found your brother," he said gently. "It was Morgan's tip that started us looking. I'm afraid . . . well . . ."

"He's dead?" Her eyes were grave. "Do you know what . . how it happened?"

"No, he's not dead, but he's in bad shape. Somehow he must have tangled with Gus. He took a bad beating and he's been lying in the hospital unconscious. They found him only last night when a couple of wino friends of his came to the police. They'd found him and taken him in, figured he'd just been drunk and taken a beating. When he didn't come out of it, they got scared."

"He's all right? I mean . . . is he conscious?"

"Yeah, he's conscious, but I won't lie to you. He's in bad shape." Mooney glanced at Kip. "He spotted you. He'd been hiding out, away from his old hangouts, tailing Villani and his boys. He saw you in a grease joint across from that warehouse."

Kip took Marilyn's arm. "Let's get out of here."

When they had walked almost to his car, he said thoughtfully, "That's why those eyes looked familiar to me. They were your eyes. Like yours, anyway. He was sitting there all the time and must have heard me asking questions, but didn't know why I was interested. We'll go see him."

"Tomorrow," she said. "He'll be asleep now, and the sleep will do him more good than anything else. In the meanwhile, could you go for a drink?"

"Well," he admitted, "I could . . . if you twisted my arm."

"Consider it twisted," she said gently.